An Edgartown Christmas

SISTERS OF EDGARTOWN

KATIE WINTERS

Chapter One

For years after the fact, Jennifer Conrad would remember her son's wedding to beautiful Stacy Vender as the last, glittering moment before everything in the lives of the Sisters of Edgartown changed forever.

It was November 20th. The day had been crossed-out and highlighted on every one of Jennifer's calendars, from the bird-themed one at the Frosted Delights bakery to the official online document at her social media firm. November 20th was the day her son planned to pledge his life to Stacy Vender: just two kids, really, at twenty-three and twenty-one, with their entire lives stretched before them and enough optimism to get them through.

The weeks leading up to the event were a blur of chaos. Jennifer hunkered down and set her sights on the goal in mind, grateful that Stacy's mother was the full captain of their ship, with the welcome assistance of Charlotte Hamner, one of the island's most successful wedding planners. It would be a rather elaborate affair, with two-hundred and seventeen guests RVSP-ing, yes. Stacy had an elegant, multi-tiered wedding dress, which she'd selected from a vintage boutique in Oak Bluffs. It was said to have been worn by Vineyard royalty circa 1962. With her vibrant blonde locks and her enormous doe eyes, she could have been Marilyn Monroe's twin. Everyone said so.

The hour before the ceremony, Jennifer stopped by the bridal room to greet Stacy's mother, who was red-faced and inarticulate, a contrast to Stacy's bridesmaids who scuttled around the ornate room taking selfies and sipping champagne.

"Is everything all set?" Jennifer asked warmly.

Stacy's mother gripped Jennifer's elbow and dragged her to the corner of the room. She gulped in an effort to ease her anxiety. "It was really difficult to get Stacy's dress zipped," she whispered.

"Oh gosh. I'm sure with all these celebrations, that's understandable. But she looks beautiful," Jennifer commented. She was unfortunately accustomed to mothers who put such undue body pressure on their daughters. Self-hatred was so often passed from generation to generation, mother to daughter. Jennifer hadn't had a daughter, but she'd seen the hand-off often enough.

"And she spent almost all morning in the bathroom," Stacy's mom continued, her eyes bulging. "She may be sick, I think, although I'm not sure."

"It's understandable to get sick on your wedding day. Nerves can do the strangest things to you. All those people are coming from all over the country," Jennifer countered.

But Stacy's mother wouldn't drop it. "My daughter and I have never had the kind of relationship where you tell each other everything. But there's something different about her— something, like a glow of some kind. I just can't seem to put my finger on it."

Jennifer's jaw dropped. She peered across the room at Stacy as she fluffed her over-the-top skirt out from her still-thin waist. A glass of untouched champagne bubbled on the armoire beside her as her bridesmaids gushed. The makeup artist charged through them with an eyebrow pencil lifted. "Just a touch deeper with the brows, I think," the woman said. "To give you that real Marilyn Monroe feel."

"You think maybe she's—" Jennifer whispered.

"I don't know. I really don't," Stacy's mother nearly screeched, but they were thinking the exact same thing. "But gosh, isn't it too much to bear? Our babies are marrying today, only to possibly have babies of their own! Some mothers have to wait years for their first grandchild—all that talk of wanting to 'enjoy' the honeymoon phase before car seats and diapers. I say; have it all at once. We in the Vender family and you in your family have enough love to go around." She then lowered her voice to add, "And I say that even though you and Joel have divorced. I hope Stacy and Nick know that's not a viable option for them."

Jennifer's cheeks flushed with heat. Perhaps she wasn't so keen on becoming Stacy's mother's friend. Already, if it was true Stacey was pregnant with their first child, she found herself an adversary. Stacey's mother was: a woman apt to take up way more of this baby's time than Jennifer, if only because she no longer worked and was the mother of the bride.

Stacy's mother rushed off to tend to a bridesmaid, who had splashed champagne across the breast of her gown. Jennifer plunged back into the hallway as her thoughts raced. *A grand-*

mother? At forty-one, nearly forty-two? It had already been a struggle in the previous few years to share Nick with Stacy; their one-on-one hang-outs had dwindled, as Nick had brought Stacy along to nearly every event. The spark between the two of them was infectious. But Jennifer knew she and Nick could never really go back to the old days when she'd felt they were a team.

Joel hovered in his suit outside the grand hall of the popular Harbor View Hotel, located just outside of Edgartown, where the ceremony was set to take place. His hands were shoved in his pockets, and he slumped his shoulders forward, lost in his own thoughts. For a moment, Jennifer could only imagine he was the teenage boy she'd fallen head-over-heels for. For decades, it had been Jennifer and Joel, Joel and Jennifer. When they'd both admitted their love wasn't enough to sustain their marriage any longer, their hearts had shattered even in the midst of their brave step forward. They'd since both found love with others, a remarkable thing.

"Hey, you." Jennifer nudged Joel with a sharp elbow. He leaped up, startled.

"Oh. Hi. I was looking for you," he told her. His smile was mischievous and reminiscent of another time. "Can you believe today's the big day?"

"Hardly." Jennifer pressed her lips together for a moment. She burned to tell him the pregnancy gossip but held it inside. The news felt like a trapped bird in a cage. "Our baby's getting married."

"Feels like just yesterday..." Joel replied sheepishly.

"It only feels like yesterday that we learned he'd skipped school to go to a concert in Boston and had to ground him for two months? I was thinking the same thing," Jennifer teased.

"Yes, I should have known better than to get all nostalgic today," Joel returned, palming the back of his neck as he scanned the room once more.

Jennifer's eyes grew heavy with tears. It took all her strength to hold them at bay. "I loved every minute of raising him with you, you know."

Joel locked eyes with her from the side. "Ditto."

Derek, Jennifer's boyfriend, stepped into the foyer after that. He was dressed in an immaculate, Italian-cut suit, and his dark curls were ruffled from the sharp November winds. He greeted them warmly and placed a kiss on Jennifer's cheek. Just that year, his own daughter, Emma, had married, which had been a particularly emotional moment. Only two years ago, his wife had died and left a crater the size of the moon on his heart. Jennifer prayed their love acted as a sort of bandage over whatever that horror meant. She'd watched Mila go through a similar torment in the wake of her husband, Peter's death. All you could do was keep going, dragging your mangled limbs and heart and mind along with you.

Jennifer, Derek, Joel, and Joel's girlfriend, Renée, all sat together in the front row on the groom's side. All two-hundred and seventeen guests arrived, one after another, a flurry of gorgeous Islanders from Nick and Stacy's beautiful existence together as relative king-and-queen of Edgartown High School. Each face was lined with a memory for Jen: of basketball and baseball games and PTO events and school trips. She and Joel had been remarkably involved in their son's life— normally the first-listed chaperone at every school function. She waved at a young woman from Nick's class who carried a baby on her hip and grinned back. Somehow, Jennifer had found it easy to become an adult herself, moving from her life at her parents' to her life with Joel and Nick. It wasn't so easy to watch the next generation take the same steps.

The string quintet swept through a side door to arrange themselves at the five chairs toward the right-hand side of the room. They took a collective breath and placed their bows upon the strings before sweeping into Pachelbel's Canon, which would bring the bridesmaids and the groomsmen down the aisle. Jennifer had been to countless weddings and appeared as a bridesmaid in the weddings for Olivia, Mila, and Camilla. This wedding sizzled with a different adrenaline.

When Stacy appeared in her Marilyn-Monroe-inspired gown and her flowing blonde tresses, the audience rushed to their feet to honor her youth and her beauty and her hope for her fresh new life. Her father walked proudly alongside her down the aisle with a stoic expression that reminded Jennifer of her own quiet, sorrowful soul. Celebrations marked new beginnings; they also bid goodbye to the old.

Hours later, Jennifer stood at a high-top table alongside Olivia, a very pregnant Amelia, Mila, and Camilla as the reception erupted with life before them. Toward the far end of the room, Nick tossed his head back in laughter as one of his groomsmen whispered a joke in his ear.

"He looks happy. I'll give him that," Mila noted with a funny smile.

"He did it all right," Camilla returned proudly. "Marrying one of the most beautiful girls on the island and setting up his life just a few streets from his momma. How lucky are we that our kids don't want to run so far away?"

"Just another few weeks till Andrea moves here full-time," Amelia offered.

"Counting down the days," Camilla affirmed.

Olivia heaved a sigh. Her daughter, Chelsea, remained in Brooklyn with her boyfriend, Xavier, as they struggled through the romantic obstacles of "making ends meet" in one of the most expensive cities in the world.

"Oh honey," Mila remarked softly as she splayed her head over Olivia's shoulder. "My babies are gone, too. Maybe they just need to take this time alone to figure some stuff out."

"Why can't they figure it all out from the comfort of home?" Olivia asked tenderly.

Suddenly, Nick appeared before the five of them. He wore that ridiculous, mischievous, overly-handsome smile, the one he'd inherited from his father, and splayed a hand out before Jennifer.

"I don't suppose I could have this dance?"

"What a gentleman!" Olivia cried.

"Only if you can spare a moment. I know how popular you are today, my dear," Jennifer teased.

But in a moment, her much-taller, confident son had her hand in his as he whirled her across the dance floor. Jennifer's heart swept into her throat as they stepped lightly through the other revelers. How could she articulate just how much he meant to her? How could she find the words?

"I'm so proud of you, Nick," she finally mustered, looking up into his eyes.

"What for?" His laughter was infectious.

"For taking such a big step, for putting yourself out there and for choosing light instead of the darkness." Jennifer dropped her eyes as another surge of feeling beamed out from her heart.

"Both of my parents set the best example for me. Why shouldn't I follow your lead?" Nick returned with a slight shrug.

Jennifer's eyelashes fluttered. Off to the side, Stacy giggled with two bridesmaids, still without a drink in hand.

"I'm so excited to see what happens next," Jennifer admitted softly.

"Don't get ahead of yourself, Mom. We got to the wedding day. Let me just enjoy it before all that other stuff," Nick told her.

After the dance, Jennifer returned to the table with her Sisters. Mila reported that her new boyfriend, the police officer, Liam, would join them shortly, as he had to work a late shift. Anthony paraded forward to give Olivia a fresh glass of wine. Derek soon appeared and wrapped his arms around Jennifer's stomach, holding her tightly against him. And soon after, Camilla's husband, Jonathon, returned from a conversation with Joel and asked Camilla for a dance. Amelia's boyfriend, the NYC developer, Oliver, had had to leave the island that weekend to tend to affairs in the city. In the next months, he and Amelia would welcome Amelia's baby— and expectation forced him to tie up loose ends elsewhere.

Time had rushed them forward to this moment. All they could do was hold on, support one another, and open their eyes wide for whatever came next.

Chapter Two

Thanksgiving Week became a blur of roasted turkeys, stuffing, baked pies and buttery biscuits. As though the food at home wasn't enough, the Frosted Delights bakery was a flurry of activity, with hungry home-comers meeting for donuts and coffee and conversation. Jennifer sucked down copious cups of black roasted coffee and forced herself through a grueling schedule of four a.m. bakery-start-up followed by several mid-afternoon hours at the social media firm.

Thanksgiving Thursday and Black Friday, Jennifer closed the bakery in pursuit of something she hadn't had in quite some time: days of R&R. That said, Jennifer was never one to lounge around at home. When Olivia suggested the Sisters meet Friday for a bout of Black Friday shopping at the numerous boutiques across Oak Bluffs and Edgartown, the girls jumped at the chance. For some of them, Thursday had been fraught with family tension— something often served alongside the stuffing and yams at the Thanksgiving table. Friday would heal them.

It was decided that they meet at Tiffany-Ann's Boutique in downtown Edgartown at one in the afternoon on Black Friday. It was strangely warm despite the lateness of the year, and Jennifer stood in only a dark green trench, a pair of skinny jeans, a black turtleneck, and a pair of booties, poised at the edge of the sidewalk and trying her darnedest not to glance at her phone during these moments of quiet. She was the first to arrive, which was normally Amelia's thing. These days, Amelia lagged a bit due to her pregnant belly.

"There she is!" Olivia stepped out from around the corner and wrapped Jennifer in a big hug, bringing with her a new brand of perfume Jennifer didn't fully recognize.

"Wow. What's that?"

Olivia stepped back and waved a hand around herself to boost the aroma. "Chelsea got it for me from a perfume boutique in Manhattan. What do you think?"

"You're a classy city lady these days," Jennifer returned. "I can't possibly compete with that."

"Chelsea keeps me young," Olivia beamed, tucking a strand of hair behind her ear.

Amelia parked her car directly before them, aligning it parallel with the sidewalk with perfect precision. When she stepped out, her pregnant belly ballooned in front of her.

"Just so you know, girls, I can't keep up with you as well as other Black Fridays," Amelia grumbled. "And I'm mostly here for whatever snacks we get ourselves into. Maternity clothes are like bags of fabric, and my feet don't fit any shoes I like."

"I see you're in a good mood today," Jennifer teased.

A few minutes later, Andrea dropped Camilla off on the corner and gave a sturdy wave. Camilla grumbled as she waved back.

"The girl's wedding is going to kill me," she said through clenched teeth.

"Just one more week! And then it's over! Trust me. I feel a huge weight lifted now that Nick's wedding is done with," Jennifer told her.

"We have to do another dress fitting today," Camilla announced somberly. "It's at four p.m. and I can't tell you how many adjustments that dress has taken so far. It seems like a never-ending journey to perfection."

"Oh well," Amelia offered. "I'd love any chance to sit down."

"You'll go with me?" Camilla asked.

"Of course I will. You don't have to go through this alone," Olivia offered. "Plus, I have the feeling Chelsea's enjoying her new life in the city too much to ever get married, and I want to leech up some of your mother-of-the-bride joy."

"Take it," Camilla said sarcastically. "I don't want it anymore!"

The girls cackled together as a wind ripped off the Nantucket Sound and cut through the strange humidity of the overly warm day.

"Weird weather," Jennifer affirmed as she pushed her hands into her trench coat pocket.

"Where's Mila, anyway?" Camilla asked.

"I don't know. It's fifteen past," Olivia breathed. "Maybe we should call her?"

Jennifer dialed Mila's number for the millionth time in her life. As was Mila's custom, she didn't answer but immediately texted back.

MILA: Sorry! Got held up with something.

MILA: I'll call you in an hour and see where you are.

"Guess that means we should get started without her," Olivia stated. "Too bad for her. She's the most fashion-obsessed of all of us."

Mila had always been the group's in-the-know fashionista, delivering sterling advice as they'd gone through the season of life and the seasons of trends. They couldn't dress like they were twenty-two any longer— but Mila allowed them to look chic and poised regardless of the situation.

They stepped into Tiffany-Ann's Boutique and set to work at the sales' rack as a mumbling clerk asked them if they needed any assistance. She also informed Amelia where the maternity section was, which made Amelia grumble inwardly before thanking her.

"The world is so excited that I'm as huge as a whale," she announced as the clerk rushed off to help someone else. "But who am I kidding? Not like my body will pop back to its pre-baby shape like before." She snapped her fingers.

"You know we'll go to endless spin classes with you in solidarity," Jennifer told her.

"I, for one, don't think you should worry at all about your body," Camilla said as she collected three of the same sweaters in different colors, hanging them across her finger. "You're bringing a baby into the world. It's the most beautiful and natural thing you can do. Andrea destroyed my body for a little while. Against all odds, I still love her to pieces, and I ended up loving my body even more through the process." Jennifer said.

Amelia rolled her eyes playfully. "You always have to say the kindest thing, Camilla. Give it a rest sometimes, huh?"

"Can't help it," Camilla returned as she lifted all three sweaters in orange, brown, and yellow. "Which color do you think suits me best?"

"None of them," Amelia returned as the others burst into laughter. "What? I thought we were all about honesty here."

"Honesty appreciated," Camilla affirmed as she snuck the sweater back on the rack. "We've been through too much for you girls to let me walk around in an ugly sweater."

"We would never do that to each other," Jennifer assured her, then leafed through a collection of black dresses toward the corner.

Around two in the afternoon, they checked back in with Mila to learn that she was still in the midst of a "tumultuous" fight with her daughter, Isabelle.

"Oh gosh. Thanksgiving really brings out the worst in people sometimes," Olivia said timidly as they stepped out of the first boutique and headed for another down the block. "You should have heard what my mom said to my dad last night over pie. Basically, she insinuated that all he does is sit around the house all day. I mean, the man worked hard his entire life. Maybe he deserves a rest?"

"I sometimes remember when I needled Joel. When I heard myself, I was like, 'Have I turned into my mother?' But really, I think picking and prodding at someone like that is more of a reflection of yourself rather than them. Joel was always a magnificent husband. I just wasn't happy anymore, and stuff like, you know, the lawn not being mowed correctly made me angrier than it should have."

It was another classic day of seemingly endless girl talk. As they fell into an easy silence at the next boutique, Jennifer thought about how these conversations had shifted over the years. In their teenage days, back when Michelle had still been with them, their conversations had circled around what to wear to prom and which boys they wanted to take them there. They had discussed the best places to drive to make out without being caught. They'd swapped jeans and nail polishes and magazines, the only real currency they'd had. It was the privilege of Jennifer's life to be allowed such endless conversations with her girls.

"How's Nick doing, anyway?" Olivia muttered through the hangers in the dress section. "Did he ever confirm what Stacy's mom thinks...?"

Jennifer had confessed the Stacy pregnancy secret to her girls several days previous.

"Not yet," Jennifer replied mischievously.

"I didn't see her take a single drink of alcohol throughout the entire reception," Camilla confirmed.

"And she has a glow about her. Something more than the wedding glow," Amelia added. "As a pregnant woman, I have a sixth sense about this."

"A grandmother!" Jennifer buzzed her lips distractedly. "At the same time, you become a mother for the first time."

"Maybe the baby can call you Nana or something," Camilla said playfully. "You're no, Grandma. Not looking the way you do — barely thirty-five and in skinny jeans."

Jennifer blushed. "Mila's esthetician salon has been a real skin-saver."

"I wish she would get here. She's missing out on all the good gossip," Olivia moaned. "And we seem to miss out on each other over the holidays. There are so many things to do and presents to wrap and parents to fight with. Gosh, that reminds me. I heard from Tyler the other day. More apologies for his lack of involvement during Chelsea's childhood. It seems like his new baby has really triggered a lot of memories for him, especially because nobody's letting him off the hook this time."

"Did you tell him you haven't invented a time machine yet?" Camilla blurted.

Olivia laughed. "Honestly, him thinking about my feelings for the first time maybe ever is revolutionary. It makes me think the world isn't as lost as I always thought it was."

"Besides, you have Anthony, now," Jennifer countered. "Finally, a man who treats you the way you deserve."

"That reminds me," Camilla chimed in. "If we're going to be at Something Blue later anyway..."

Olivia's cheeks burned red with embarrassment. She pressed a hand over her stomach and said, "I don't know if I'm up for trying anything on..."

"Come on, Olivia. You only get married for the second time once," Amelia teased.

Olivia rolled her eyes. "Okay, but I told you, I want something understated. Something that says..."

"That says you've finally found you're happily ever after?" Jennifer finished her sentence. "I think we can figure that out."

The four of them retreated from the second boutique with

only three bags between them. They hadn't made many big purchases yet; rather, the clothes and the shoes and the jewelry seemed more like decoration around their companionship. On the way to the bridal shop, Jennifer paused in front of a shoe store for two terribly strained minutes as she gazed at a pair of three-hundred dollar heels in the window. "They're screaming my name. I could hear them saying, *'Jennifer! Hey!'* from all the way down the block."

"But where are you going to wear them?" Camilla asked.

Jennifer blushed. "I don't know, especially because I might be a grandmother soon. No grandmother would be caught dead in heels like that."

"Don't be ridiculous," Amelia teased. "You work hard. If you want those shoes, you should get them."

Mila called them just then, right in the nick of time. Jennifer lifted her phone in excitement.

"Are you coming? I'm trying to decide about these shoes and I need you here as the devil on the shoulder."

"Still not out," Mila grumbled. "I hate it. I hate missing out on quality time with my girls."

Jennifer turned as another wicked yet strangely warm wind cast itself across her cheeks. "You know we understand. It's just sad, is all and I have no idea when we'll all be together again."

"Until your birthday, of course," Mila affirmed.

Every year on December 15th, the five of them always gathered to celebrate Jennifer and Michelle's birthday. They made all their favorite greasy-delight foods from high school and had a sort of conversation with Michelle, telling her all the events she'd missed from the previous year and how much they still missed her (so much that it still hurt).

"That's almost three weeks away," Jennifer moaned.

"Oh gosh. You're not going to give me attitude, too, because I just can't handle it." Mila teased.

"No, no. We're just teasing you, honey. Take care of what you need to take care of. In the meantime, we're taking Olivia to look at wedding dresses!"

"You're kidding. That's totally unfair," Mila countered. "Tell her not to pick something for sure until I'm there. I know you girls. You get all in your heads about fashion decisions sometimes and I have to swoop in and save the day."

"Someone's a little high and mighty," Jennifer returned.

"You know it's true. Olivia could walk out of there wearing a Cinderella ballgown."

"Oh ye of so little faith," Jennifer said with a laugh.

When they reached Something Blue, it was three-fifteen, which gave them a full forty-five minutes to hunt for a dress prior to Andrea's arrival for her fitting. Olivia cowered in the corner while Jennifer explained to the store clerk that Olivia planned to marry sometime next year.

"But I'm old! I'm forty-one!" Olivia cried.

"Don't be silly," the clerk told her. "You deserve a dress as much as anyone else."

As Olivia explained her style to the clerk, Charlotte Hamner and her sister, Claire, entered the boutique, each wearing vibrant smiles. Claire operated her own flower shop in Oak Bluffs while wedding-planner Charlotte had several more weddings over the span of the next weeks after a particularly wild year post-Ursula Pennington's celebrity wedding. Since then, Jennifer had taken Ursula on as a social media client and had been privy to her socialite world.

"Hi there," Charlotte greeted brightly. "Your son's wedding went off without a hitch. It was such a beautiful day."

"So many thanks to you for that," Jennifer returned. "We've got ourselves yet another bride if you can believe it."

Olivia rolled her eyes flippantly mid-way through her conversation with the clerk.

"It's so exciting! Oh, you must have it at The Hesson House when it reopens," Charlotte said.

"That's the plan. A perfect way to start the next era of the hotel," Jennifer affirmed.

"Nothing like a wedding to bring about enough hope to keep going," Charlotte offered dreamily. "But don't mind me. I'm just about the biggest sap in the world."

"We need that kind of energy around here." Jennifer beamed as the clerk led Olivia toward a small selection of vintage-looking, classical gowns.

"Seems one of your group is missing today," Charlotte noted as she scanned across the foursome.

"Mila couldn't get away from her kids," Jennifer explained. "But she'll join us later. Most likely for the wine and complaints about whatever Isabelle and Zane put her through. They just started at college and, well, I think there are growing pains on all fronts."

Charlotte puffed out her cheeks. "I dread the day my Rachel heads off to college. I keep teasing the idea that she just stays here with me to work on the business. She already knows so many of the ins and outs, considering she's been my helper since she was maybe ten or eleven. She's certainly got the wedding genes. I hope she never tries to actually get married, though. Not sure my heart could take it."

"Tell me about it," Camilla returned as her own daughter breezed through the door, delivering a sterling, bride-ready smile. "I think my heart might just explode into a million pieces. Joy is painful like that."

Chapter Three

"I think we should stick to the old standard. Rosé, rosé, all day," Olivia grumbled as she assessed the wine list at the nearby Edgartown Wine Bar. They'd forced her through five itchy vintage gowns, including one with a veil that weighed approximately ten pounds. When she'd insinuated that she was just their clown for the afternoon, they'd howled with laughter and decided to try again another day. They had nothing but time— and now, she needed a drink. Stat.

"Let's get two bottles," Camilla announced. "That fitting nearly destroyed me. Andrea got so finicky lately. She's not exactly bridezilla, but she's merging into villa-territory."

Jennifer chuckled inwardly. In truth, it had been almost shocking to witness Andrea's occasional sharp-edged remarks toward her mother throughout the fitting. Andrea and Camilla had had their hardships over the years, especially the previous year or so when Camilla had kicked Jonathon to the curb. Since then, they'd patched up their family to near-perfection— with the occasional hanging string of resentment. That was what families were: imperfect.

"Still no sign from Mila?" Amelia sipped her bubbly water timidly and eyed Jennifer.

"Nothing. We might have to count her out for the day," Jennifer cautioned.

Amelia's eyes watered. Hurriedly, she wiped them away and muttered, "Gosh, I'm just a barrel of emotions lately. So what? Mila can't come. Why does it feel like the end of the world?"

"Because you're worried you won't see us when you have your baby," Camilla offered. "Which is silly— we'll be there at your beck and call, just like you were when we all had our babies."

"One by one, I watched you all become mothers and thought..." Amelia trailed off as another round of tears took hold of her. "Oh boy. I'm just pathetic."

The waiter arrived to take their wine and small-plate orders.

"Remarkable that I can be hungry again after yesterday," Olivia noted with a laugh. "The human body is amazing."

"I know! I ate two pieces of pie last night and now I'm like, 'Yeah, I could probably eat that whole cheese plate,'" Camilla returned, chuckling.

The wine arrived along with a selection of stinky cheeses, various types of freshly-baked bread, olives, vegetable dips, hummus, and stuffed mushrooms. Amelia moaned as she bit into a stuffed mushroom.

"Do you think kids like stuffed mushrooms?" she asked as she chewed. "I'm getting nervous about a life filled with chicken nuggets and juice boxes."

"I don't think you can train children to automatically like small plates at wine bars," Jennifer teased.

"I think if anyone could do it, it's Amelia," Camilla countered.

Outside, the light had dimmed to a strange and sinister greyish purple. Five-thirty p.m. and only weeks until Christmas crafted a festive spirit within the wine bar, with friends and relatives gathering for boisterous conversation as the speakers hummed Christmas music. Jennifer checked her phone for some sign from Mila, but found only a text from Joel, whom she hadn't heard from over Thanksgiving.

JOEL: Hope you had a wonderful holiday with your fam!

JOEL: And I hope you and the girls are having your traditional Black Friday shopping spree.

JOEL: All my love.

"Who are you texting?" Camilla asked.

"Joel," Jennifer responded instantly.

"Gosh, you two are like the poster children for divorce," Camilla returned. "As a woman who nearly got divorced myself, I can't imagine it. Jonathon was like my number-one villain."

"And now look at you two. All lovey-dovey all over again," Jennifer teased.

"He's just smitten about the wedding. He can't believe his little girl's all grown up. He told me he's terrified about walking her down the aisle because he had a dream that he tripped on the way and ruined the ceremony," Camilla continued.

Just then, Camilla's own phone began to buzz. She grabbed it from her purse, muttering that she'd "forgotten to turn it off." But a brief glance at the screen gave her pause.

"What's wrong?" Olivia asked as she placed a square of cheese on her tongue.

"I have to get this." Camilla placed the phone to her ear and changed her tone to a harsher one. "Rita? What's up?"

Shock poured over Camilla's face. She grew rigid and strange as she listened. Jennifer's heart dropped into the acid of her stomach. Something was very wrong. With Andrea? Jonathon? What? Hadn't Camilla been through enough?

"I'm on my way now," Camilla blared to whoever was on the phone. "I'll be right there."

Camilla's eyes filled with tears. She threw her phone into her purse as her limbs shook.

"That was the hospital. Mila... Mila's there."

Jennifer's ears began to ring. "What? What happened?"

"I don't know. Car accident? Car accident." Camilla said the words as though they were a different language. She scuttled up to stand and gaped at the window, where the violent late-November winds tore through the trees that lined the street.

"We need to pay!" Amelia hollered at the passing waiter before shuffling through her wallet to grab two fifty-dollar bills. "This should cover it. Let's go."

The four-some raced out into the street, where they crammed into Amelia's car. Traffic was horrific, as everyone who was everyone wanted to nibble on the sights and sounds of Holiday in Edgartown. The radio kicked off with a speech from some local politician, wishing everyone happy holidays. Amelia pressed the OFF button to leave them in silence as she eased out of the parking spot and into traffic. Everything seemed to move in slow motion.

"Did they say anything else?" Olivia asked, her voice clearly panicked.

"Just that Mila has to go into surgery," Camilla returned firmly.

"Surgery?" Jennifer and Amelia cried in unison.

"I'm not there. I don't know anything else," Camilla blurted angrily.

"Should we call her parents? Liam?" Jennifer asked, not know what to do. "Were her kids with her?"

At this, her heart surged with fear. Isabelle and Zane were Mila's entire universe. If they'd gotten into an accident together...

The potential of that was too difficult to think of.

"I don't know anything else," Camilla continued. "Let's just get there, for goodness sake."

"Let's not be angry with each other!" Amelia cried from the driver's seat.

Silence fell as they stopped and started their way through the streets of Edgartown to finally buzz along the main road between Edgartown and Oak Bluffs. Although they'd driven this route perhaps a hundred and fifty thousand times, this particular time felt haunted and slow, like a road that would stretch on and on into the distance without giving them their destination.

"I can't believe this," Olivia breathed, saying what they all clearly thought.

They'd already lost one of them— Michelle, on that fateful night when they'd only been seventeen years old.

They couldn't afford to lose anyone else.

It wasn't fair. None of this was fair.

As they surged toward the hospital, Jennifer tried Mila's mother's cell. It went straight to voicemail. Mila's mother's recorded voicemail explained she and her husband were away for the week on a trip to Europe, where they didn't have cell service.

"I forgot Mila mentioned that," Jennifer breathed as she ended the failed call. "What a horrible time for them to be away."

"Contact her through social media?" Camilla suggested. "They'll want to come back as soon as they can."

The hospital emergency waiting room was just as busy as the Edgartown Wine Bar but with a far different, much darker energy. A family of four waited in the corner with red-tinged eyes. A toddler screamed from the arms of his mother as she wandered up and down the aisles of chairs—a ten-year-old kid with a bright mop of blonde hair held onto his clearly broken arm, awaiting care.

Camilla charged directly for the on-hand secretary, who greeted her immediately while the other three waited behind, shifting their weight. Olivia suggested Amelia sit down, but Amelia gave no indication that she heard her.

Camilla's conversation was held in low, earnest tones. When she turned back, her eyes were hollowed out. She whisked the girls to a far corner as she described what she now knew.

"Mila and Isabelle were the only ones in the car," she explained. "Zane left the island this afternoon, but apparently, Isabelle stuck around for some reason. They crashed into a pole outside of Edgartown. Mila didn't notice a car coming and had to swerve at the last second. Isabelle has some injuries but nothing major. She's receiving care right now."

"I'm one of her emergency contacts," Jennifer blurted.

Camilla nodded. "Then I think you'll be able to head in to see her shortly."

Jennifer dug her teeth into her lower lip and stared at the doorway between the waiting room and the rest of the white-washed halls of the hospital. Amelia finally did stagger to the nearest chair, where she splayed a hand over her stomach and focused on her breathing.

"Maybe we should take Amelia home," Olivia murmured.

"I heard that," Amelia called. "And there's no way in hell I'm going anywhere."

"Does anyone have Liam's number?" Camilla muttered.

"Maybe the police station would have it?" Jennifer suggested. She dialed the non-emergency number and received the secretary, who explained that Liam was off-duty and off the island for the weekend visiting family in Boston. Jennifer explained it was an emergency and imperative that she reached him, and the secretary gave her his information with reluctance. When she dialed Liam's number, however, she again reached his voicemail.

Instead of leaving a voicemail with the potential to be ignored, Jennifer texted him.

JENNIFER: Hey Liam. It's Jennifer Conrad. Could you give me a call tonight? It's an emergency.

An hour had already passed when Camilla disappeared to the break room to grab them coffee, tea, and granola bars, which they ate slowly just for something to do. Finally, a doctor appeared to tell Camilla that Isabelle's emergency contact could enter the room to visit her. Jennifer leaped up and traced the path down the menacingly bright hallway, all the way into the belly of the hospital.

Isabelle tried to sit bolt-upright as Jennifer entered but soon collapsed back onto her pillow. The nurse in the room scolded her.

"I told you. No quick movements."

Isabelle grumbled inwardly as tears formed in the corners of her eyes. There were minor scratches across her cheeks and forehead, and her left arm was wrapped in a cast. There, so small upon the bright white hospital bed, she seemed the spitting image of her mother at her age. Mila had been something else: the most beautiful, long-legged, long-tressed cheerleader, who'd had all the boys wrapped around her finger.

"Oh, honey." Jennifer stepped forward and tried to hug Isabelle tenderly without mussing her bandages.

"Jennifer..." Isabelle's voice broke. "I don't even know..." Cries erupted from her throat as she crumpled into herself.

"It's okay, honey. It's okay. You're okay," Jennifer whispered. She perched on the chair beside the bed and peered up at Isabelle as she stroked her hand lovingly. How perfectly she remembered the day when Isabelle and Zane had been born! Peter, their father, had been nothing but nervous energy, skittering across the hospital telling everyone he'd had twins.

"It's not. It's all my fault." Isabelle's voice was thick with tears.

"What happened?"

Isabelle clenched her eyes tightly closed. "We fought all week. I told her that I didn't want to go back to school. I was head-hunted by a major model agency in New York City and dammit, that's what I want to do. I already went to look at apartments. But Mom told me that was out of the question. I even planned to go to the city tonight to meet with the agency. She wouldn't let me get on the ferry."

Jennifer could hear the strain in Isabelle's words. They sizzled with anger and fear and sorrow. She was a whirlwind of emotion.

"She wanted to keep me here this weekend to talk some sense into me, I guess," Isabelle continued. "We dropped Zane off at the ferry and then drove back to Edgartown. And then— I don't even know what happened. She was ranting about something. She was so angry. I'd never seen her like that. Telling me that I owe it to myself and to Dad to go back to school..." Isabelle stuttered. "And then, that car came out of nowhere, and we crashed... I don't remember much after that until the ambulance came."

Jennifer's heart shattered. She continued to stroke Isabelle's hand as a way to remind her she remained on solid ground.

"They told me she's in surgery," Isabelle breathed. "And I remember what she looked like before they strapped her into the gurney. It was so awful, Jen. I'll never forget it. Not ever."

All the blood drained from Isabelle's face. Jennifer willed herself to keep her sanity, just for Isabelle's sake. In reality, this was a nightmare from which she prayed they would soon wake.

Chapter Four

Isabelle's eyes fluttered closed a half-hour after Jennifer arrived to her room. Jennifer stepped into the hallway, where she leaned against the plain white wall and burst into tears. She could envision the anger between the two spitfire women. There was Isabelle, on the brink, in her mind, of becoming a world-renowned model. There was Mila, forced to stand in the way of this potential, if only for the good of her daughter's education. Jennifer could comprehend the weight of both sides. She could practically hear the volatile words hurled from one side of the car to the other before the anger culminated in a horrific crash.

How useless. How stupid.

Camilla appeared at the far end of the hallway and lifted a hand to wave. Jennifer rushed toward her and flung her arms around her. For a moment, they held onto one another as though they would drown otherwise. When Jennifer lifted her chin from Camilla's shoulder, she explained what Isabelle had told her.

"How awful. You told her it wasn't her fault? That these things happen?"

"Of course," Jennifer breathed. "But she wouldn't listen. I'm sure this is all really confusing for her; her being in a hospital room and not knowing what to do with herself while her mother's in surgery. I can't even imagine what is going through Isabelle's head."

"I just spoke with another nurse about Mila's injuries," Camilla murmured. "She said another three to five hours of surgery."

"Oh my God. I don't even know how we'll get through that time," Jennifer breathed.

They locked eyes for a long moment as memories passed between them. Obviously, the pain of this night resembled the pain of that long-ago night, when they'd waited up for hours to hear if Michelle had been found. The news hadn't been good news. Maybe this wouldn't be, either.

They had to mentally prepare for the worst while they hoped for the best.

Back in the waiting room, Olivia expressed interest in getting "the hell out of there" while they waited.

"I don't want to go far," she insisted. "Just away from the energy in this room."

"Let's just go hang out in my car," Amelia suggested.

"I need a drink," Jennifer blurted.

The others agreed. Amelia said she'd even jump for a diet cola, which she normally resisted on her constant quest to be healthy for the baby. They headed out into the warm wind, where they slid into Amelia's car and drove to the nearest liquor store.

Jennifer and Camilla hopped out and entered the overly illuminated store, where the clerk watched a bad movie on a laptop.

"Evening," he greeted, not even looking up from his computer.

Jennifer echoed, "Evening" in return, although she had absolutely no idea what time it was. They selected several bottles of wine, a couple of cans of diet cola, plastic cups, some salty and sugary snacks, and piled everything out on the counter.

"Are you ladies having a party?" the clerk asked as he rang through the items.

"Something like that," Camilla told him somberly. Jennifer was glad she'd responded, as she didn't have the strength.

They returned to the mostly empty hospital parking lot, where they cozied up, poured the wine, and played soft songs from the speakers. For a long while, nobody knew what to say; words were never really enough, which they all knew, and anything said without thought behind it would seem even more empty and useless. The wine they'd purchased was about four hundred percent less quality when compared to the wine they'd had at the wine bar, which seemed to suit the mood.

"How's your diet soda?" Camilla finally asked Amelia.

Amelia gave a wry laugh. "To be honest with you? I can hardly taste it."

"I feel the same about the wine," Olivia murmured. "Gosh. I just can't believe we're doing this."

Nobody said it, but you could feel the word she wanted to say hovering through the air.

I can't believe we're doing this again.

Jennifer slightly remembered the existence of Derek two hours after their arrival at the hospital. She'd told him she would be home that evening late, as she had plans with the girls all day. She now hopped out of the car to call him. When he heard the news, his voice grew sinister and strange.

"I'll be there as soon as I can."

"Don't worry about it, Derek. There's nothing you can do."

"I would really feel better if I was close by, is all," he told her.

Just after, Liam called from what sounded like the most raucous bar in all of Boston.

"I can't hear you!" he called over the hubbub.

"Can you go somewhere else? Somewhere quieter?" Jennifer pressed a finger against her ear as her heart threatened to burst through her chest. This was one of the hardest calls she'd ever had to make. How awful to deliver such news like this. No intimacy.

"Hi, Jen. What's up?" Liam's voice was jagged and strange. Her text had freaked him out.

Jennifer decided to bite the bullet and get it over with.

"Liam, we're at the hospital. Mila was in an accident and she's currently in surgery."

"Christ. What happened?" he asked, then went quiet for a moment. Still in the background came the cries from a nearby bar. "I'll be back as soon as I can."

"We've got it covered. We'll see you when you get here," Jennifer told him.

"I know that. I know." His voice was suddenly high-pitched and strained. "It's not like I want to be here now... I can catch the last ferry."

Abruptly, he hung up the phone and left Jennifer out in the whipping winds of the parking lot, alone. She slid back into the car, where Camilla topped off her wine. Jennifer announced that both Derek and Liam would be with them shortly. Jonathon and Anthony were both apparently already on their way.

"Oliver's coming back tomorrow. No way I'm asking him to drive back tonight," Amelia said softly. "I'm terrified for him to make that drive now."

No one spoke for a moment. It suddenly occurred to Jennifer just how dangerous what each and every one of them did every day out on the road. Just the act of sitting in the driver's seat was an act of risk. She grabbed her phone hurriedly and texted Nick. She needed him to know she loved him. She needed him to know she would be there for him always.

JENNIFER: Hi, honey. Mila's in the hospital after a bad accident.

JENNIFER: I just wanted to let you know.

JENNIFER: Love you so much. So happy you and Stacy are happy and that you have each other. I hope you know how rare that is.

Derek appeared out from the shadows of the dark parking lot. He carried several boxes of pizza. Jennifer rolled down the window and called him over. He lifted the pizza boxes higher and grinned at the four of them, all stuffed in the car like sardines with a wine mission.

"I should have known I'd find you all together like this," he commented gently as he placed the pizza boxes in the space between Jennifer and Camilla in the backseat.

"You're our knight in shining armor," Camilla told him. "The last thing we thought about was eating a proper meal."

He saluted them. "I'm here as backup. No worries about any of your food or drink needs."

Jennifer's stomach twisted at the sight of the greasy cheese meal. Camilla took a bite and chewed thoughtfully as her eyes scanned the darkness outside the vehicle. Derek beckoned for Jen to speak to him for a moment. As she stepped from the vehicle, she felt disassociated.

Derek rubbed her back and cradled her as she shook against him.

"You girls are so strong," he breathed into her ear. "Much stronger than any woman I've met in my life. You're there for one another in everything you do. Mila senses you out here. She knows you're pulling for her."

Jennifer's chin quivered. She wanted to tell him how little he could possibly understand. Of course, he'd heard the stories of Michelle and learned of the devastation of her passing. That wasn't the same as living through it. Her heart suddenly burned to see Joel again. He'd known Michelle. He and Mila had been in her life since her early teens. Suddenly, it was as though the cast of characters in the movie of her life had switched places too quickly and left her with a strange narrative.

"I'm going to go sit in my car for a while as well," Derek reported.

"That's really nice but not necessary," she told him. "Really, we've got pizza and wine and each other. We don't need anything else."

Derek's eyes were hard. "I don't want to push myself on you. I just want to be here just in case. It's all I can do. No way can I sit at home wondering when you'll get home. Is that clear?"

Jennifer had to give in to Derek. It was almost as though he could read her like a book. Yes: she was resistant to him now. But she could possibly need him for something later. Grief was a difficult thing to place.

Jennifer returned to the car. Olivia had switched the music to an old favorite of theirs from the nineties, "Truly Madly Deeply." They struggled to keep up with the lyrics, stumbling through, with some of them picking up words here and there only for the others to kick in when they remembered, as well. Music was the ultimate transporter. Jennifer's heart swelled with a memory of Michelle listening to that very track. It had come out the same year Michelle had drowned in 1997.

In a strange way, the women in that vehicle knew they would remember every minute of that night for the rest of their lives.

As the time ticked passed, they chewed on cooling pizza, swapped stories, discussed recent fashion trends, and marveled that Christmas was just around the corner all over again. It had been nearly a year since Jennifer's mother had had her stroke, nearly a year since Jennifer had met Derek. They tried their best not to dip into sorrowful conversions and focused instead on what had once been and how much better it had gotten in the interim.

"Derek was your ultimate enemy," Amelia pointed out. "And now he's waiting over there in his car, probably listening to some nerdy podcast, just to make sure you're okay."

Jennifer blushed. "I still sometimes get this weird itch to call Joel."

The other girls exchanged glances. Camilla shrugged.

"I think it makes sense. He was your person."

"I don't think you should doubt your feelings for Derek just because you still have underlying feelings for Joel," Amelia offered.

"It's just hard sometimes for me to admit to myself that everything has changed so much," Jennifer breathed. "And now... we're here..."

Silence fell around them again. Jennifer cursed herself inwardly for having pointed again to the trouble at hand. It took them a good five minutes before Olivia drummed up another topic— another nineties tune, "Mmm Bop," which led them to harmonize despite their hazy tears.

Around one, Liam's police sirens blared him into the parking lot at the hospital. Jennifer leaped up and waved him down, not wanting him to rush into the emergency room demanding information. He stopped his sirens and leaped from his vehicle. His cheeks were red and blotchy; his eyes cast a sorrowful look.

"How is she? Why aren't you inside?"

"We just wanted to wait it out away from the waiting room," Jennifer told him.

Derek got out of his car after that and hustled over. In recent months, he and Liam had struck up a sort of friendship, although Mila and Jennifer joked that the NYC developer and the Martha's Vineyard cop had very little in common. Still, when it came to those two, sports and beer were enough. They'd made it through countless afternoons with the girls conversing about just that.

"Hey, Liam," Derek greeted him with a somber tone. "You want to sit it out with me?"

Liam kicked out a foot as though every bit of him wanted to pace to and fro, but the strangeness of the situation held him back.

He grunted inwardly, saying, "Always tell her to be careful. Be more careful. Always."

Jennifer's heart cracked. She'd never known Mila to be an incompetent driver. Probably, with everything Liam had seen as a cop, he instilled safety in everyone around him. Probably, he never wanted his own loved ones involved when it came to such horrific things. But you couldn't plan for any of it.

"Come on, man," Derek said gently as he placed a hand on Liam's shoulder. "It won't be long now till she's out. Then we'll know more."

It would be another painful, empty hour. The girls tried their darndest to keep themselves attentive, as it was terribly easy to fall into a mental, sorrowful state. Jennifer's own train of thought could latch onto things like, "What will Isabelle and Zane do if..." and spiral after that for minutes on end. It was dangerous.

Camilla received a call just past two in the morning from one of the nurses on staff. The car became deathly quiet as they waited for news.

"I see. Yes. I see." Camilla seemed to say the same things into infinity as Jennifer held her breath. When she finally added, "Thank you," she collected her phone in her lap and closed her eyes with exhaustion.

Amelia, Olivia, and Jennifer remained still. What happened next would surely change everything.

"They managed to save her legs," Camilla whispered finally.

"Oh my God," Olivia wailed softly.

"I didn't even know her losing her legs was part of the equation..." Amelia breathed.

"They saved them, but they aren't entirely sure she'll walk

again," Camilla faltered, this time allowing her voice to break. "She's resting now and probably won't be awake till morning. But she'll live. That's what we have to focus on. Our Mila is still here."

Jennifer dropped her head on the cushion of the backseat and closed her eyes. Her mind drummed up a strange soundtrack—her father's voice as he screamed to her mother, "She's dead! She's gone! She isn't coming back!" on that long-ago fateful night and morning when Michelle had left the world forever.

Mila was still there. God had spared their Sister.

But what would the next months and years look like for Mila?

Jennifer heaved a sigh and churned her weight into the door.

"Where are you going?" Camilla whispered through tears.

"I have to go tell Liam. He has to know."

Chapter Five

The ever-competent Amelia made a very good argument for them all to return home to get some sleep. "Mila is sleeping. Isabelle is sleeping. The best we can do is get some rest ourselves so we can be here tomorrow to help out in any way we can." The other Sisters agreed with reluctance. It felt like sacrilege to be allowed to depart the hospital when one of their own was strapped to a hospital bed.

Liam was despondent. He hung outside his police car with his hands stretched over the front of it as though he planned to arrest himself. The words, *"She might not walk again,"* had triggered him into a full-on collapse. Jennifer watched from the front seat of Derek's car as Liam mumbled to himself.

"We should take him home ourselves," she whispered.

"I already asked. He wants to be alone."

"People don't always know what they need," Jennifer returned, feeling sharp-edged and out of her own body.

Derek turned to meet her eyes. He drew a hand over her hand and cupped it gently. "You're a very kind, very thoughtful person, and if Liam was one of your best friends, I would agree with you. But that man has fallen into a dark pit and only he can dig his way out of it."

At that moment, Liam leaped into his police car and screeched his tires all the way to the exit, where he careened out of sight. Jennifer's heart skipped a beat.

Derek was extra-cautious on the drive back from the hospital to the home they now shared. Jennifer had sold the house she'd raised Nick in back in the summer and moved her belongings to Derek's smaller and more artistically refined condominium. The space was oddly luxurious, with deep carpeting and hardwood floors in the dining room and kitchen. Still, it echoed without the texture of memories Jennifer's old house on Green Hollow Road had had, which occasionally made her feel hollow.

Once inside, Derek rubbed her shoulders as she drooped onto the couch. She moaned inwardly but soon found the touch annoying. She turned away from him, then a moment later, Derek entered their bedroom, removed his suit, and reappeared in a white t-shirt and boxers. He was a mix of handsomeness and vulnerability with his cerulean eyes glittering and his black hair mangy, like a rock star.

"I love you, Jen. You staying up with your friends like that until you knew about Mila's surgery… It's an act of love that just reminds me what kind of person I'm with. I'm so lucky to know you."

Jennifer wasn't prepared for such compliments. Pretty words

couldn't fix Mila's legs. They couldn't turn the clock twelve hours back to before this all had happened.

"Come to bed?" Derek breathed.

Jennifer rubbed her eyes with stiff fingers. Mila had always told her not to do that. As their forever-esthetician, she'd made it her mission to demand better skincare for all and create "wrinkle-proof" habits. How silly that all seemed now.

Jennifer lay back on the five-hundred-count sheets and stared through the dark air above their bed. Derek shifted into a deep sleep almost immediately; his breath rose and fell like a song. There was no way in hell Jen would find sleep that night. She shifted slightly to catch sight of the alarm clock on the bedside table. It read: 3:34.

If she left for the Frosted Delights Bakery in twenty minutes, she would be slightly early for the first shift. She texted Colleen; the worker meant to open the bakery that morning and explained she'd do it.

JENNIFER: Go back to sleep, Colleen!

COLLEEN: What? You're a lifesaver.

Jennifer showered in the bathroom furthest from the master bedroom. Her scrubbing took on new dimensions of violence as she wanted to rid herself of the horrors of the previous day and prepare for the new, even without a blink of sleep. When she arrived at the Frosted Delights, her hair was still wet and wrapped in a winter hat. She avoided mirrors to try to trick her mind into thinking she was ready.

There was a peacefulness being at the Frosted Delights Bakery so early on a late-autumn morning. The darkness seemed all-encompassing on the outside, a never-ending black that ate up any of the light. The luminescence within the Frosted Delights seemed the only antidote— that and the buckets and buckets of donut dough Jennifer had to swirl together to make fresh batches.

Vanilla-stuffed. Caramel-coated. Lavender-and-sea-salt. Chocolate-galore. The flavors covered everything from new-age NYC-favorites, many of which Emma reported back to her, and classic ones that never went out of style. Besides the Oak Bluffs' Sunrise Cove Bistro, which sold a fine collection of baked bread and croissants, the Frosted Delights Bakery was the most sought-after bakery on the island— the perfect mid-morning treat for everything from celebrations to rainy days.

As Jennifer stirred and baked and puffed vanilla cream into pastries, tears rained down her cheeks. The sorrow felt like a perpetual storm between her chest and her stomach. The pressure was such that she almost Googled, *"What does it feel like to have a heart attack?"* but soon stopped herself, as there was nothing as sinister as getting information from the internet about what was wrong with you health-wise. It always gave the worst news.

Just past five-fifteen, after more than an hour hard at work in the back of the bakery, there was a rap at the front window. Jennifer scuttled out in her apron and her winter hat, prepared to tell whoever stopped by that they didn't open till six-thirty, and everyone who was everyone knew that.

When she appeared in the main seating area of the bakery, however, she stopped short at a very beautiful, very comforting sight.

There, on the other side of the glass, stood a bundled-up man of six-foot-three, with wide-set eyes and a gorgeous, familiar smile.

Jennifer unlatched the door hurriedly and whipped her arms around him.

"Joel!" Even the word was alarmingly beautiful as it left her tongue. She latched onto him tightly, unwilling to let go. Another cry in a series of sobs escaped her throat, and she burrowed her head in his shoulder and prayed for herself to pull it together.

"There she is. I knew you'd be here," Joel murmured into her hair.

Jennifer beckoned for him to enter. The previous day's autumn warmth had receded and left a blistering chill. Joel stepped inside and rubbed his palms together as his brow furrowed.

"I know. I look rough," Jennifer admitted as she tapped her hat.

"No, you don't. You never do," Joel assured her. He hovered in the dark shadows of the seating area. He didn't have to say it, but he did. "I heard about Mila."

Jennifer's heart pounded. For some reason, hearing Joel say it gave the reality even more dimension. She turned to head back into the kitchen area, but Joel followed after her and whipped through the swirling kitchen door directly behind.

Jennifer hovered outside of an oven as the current batch of donuts sizzled. She couldn't bring herself to look Joel in the eye.

"It was terrible, Joel," she whispered, knowing full-well she couldn't hide anything like this from Joel Porter. "We had been waiting on her to meet us all day. And then, just like that— everything changed. We stayed outside of the hospital until we knew she made it through surgery. But it sounds like it's going to be a long road ahead."

The oven beeped. Jennifer made her way over and creaked the oven door open and removed the large slab of baked goods. The aroma waved over them, sinful and cinnamon-y. Just after its removal, another batch went in.

Joel then instructed her to sit. He poured them both cups of coffee and selected two donuts from the already-baked, already-cooled slab, both of which had a gooey vanilla cream on the inside. Jennifer sipped her coffee and tried to override her exhaustion, but she knew it was no use.

"You're going to see her today?" Joel asked softly.

Jennifer nodded. "As soon as the visiting hours begin, we'll all be there. I have no idea if she'll be awake or not, but to tell you the truth, I'm terrified. How will Mila hear the news that she might never walk again? She's been unconscious since the accident. For her, the past twelve hours haven't happened. Now she'll wake up to a nightmare."

Joel nodded. His face echoed his compassion.

"She'll need you every step of the way. That's for sure," he told her.

"Yes." Jennifer caught Joel's eyes as she took another sip of coffee. "Thank you for being here for me. Checking in on me and everything. It means a lot."

Joel shrugged. "I knew you were hurting. I couldn't just let you live in that by yourself."

"Derek tried to help. He was really sweet. I just couldn't help but think, well, he hasn't been around all these years. Maybe he doesn't really get it."

"Maybe you need to give him the benefit of the doubt," Joel

offered softly. "Because I get the sense he really loves you. As jealous as that sometimes makes me..."

"You? Joel Porter? Jealous?" She was surprised she had the strength to tease him.

"I know. It's never been seen before," Joel affirmed. "But it happened. Nick's wedding, actually. I was like, who is that handsome man dancing with my wife? And then it all hit me again." He gave a half-shrug, then added, "I know it was for the best, but sometimes the best is just a little bit sad."

Jennifer nodded and dropped her eyes once more. Outside, another person wrapped their knuckles against the glass.

"What in the heck..."

"I got it."

Joel leaped up as Jennifer called out, "Tell them we don't open till six-thirty!"

But at a moment, Joel reappeared with another familiar and beautiful sight: Jennifer's son, Nick. Jennifer jumped up to hug him as another sob overtook her.

"Aren't you a sight for sore eyes!"

Nick was now a man with a man's strength. This meant his hug was nearly as good as his father's hug— warm and powerful, the kind that made you remember you stood on solid ground.

"You okay?" Nick asked as Jennifer stepped back.

"Oh, sure. I'll be okay," Jennifer murmured as her eyesight blurred. She then spun around to gather Nick's favorite chocolate-glazed donut and a cup of coffee, which she sat before him at the table.

"I can't believe I have my two guys here," she said gently. "I can't even remember the last time it was just the three of us."

Nick sipped his coffee. "Dad texted me about the accident. There was no way I'd be anywhere else."

Jennifer's heart lifted. She hadn't seen much of Nick since the wedding, as he and Stacy had admitted they needed a "social" break after greeting two-hundred and seventeen guests. He'd been around for only a little while on Thanksgiving before meeting up with Joel later in the day.

"How's Stacy?" Jennifer asked although she was grateful Stacy wasn't there.

Nick dropped his eyes for a moment. The corners of his lips curved slightly into a smile.

"Maybe this isn't the perfect time to tell you this," he began, before stuttering, "But she's pregnant. Around three months. It's finally time to tell people."

The potential news of this had freaked Jennifer out only a week before at Nick's wedding. Now, confirmation of it felt like a bright light in the darkness. She jumped up and kissed Nick on the cheek as Joel banged his fist on the table.

"A grandfather? Are you sure that's what you want me to be?" Joel demanded as he, too, hugged his son.

Nick laughed outright. "You'll be wonderful."

Joel's eyes shone with excitement. "You and me, Jen— grandparents. Can you imagine? What do you think of that?"

Jennifer's stomach tensed with a mix of fear and joy. "Guess I'd better learn how to knit, huh?"

"Naw. You've got the baking thing down. That's good enough," Nick told her.

Chapter Six

Jennifer's mother, Ariane, and Colleen, the other baker, arrived just past eight-thirty that morning to take over the reins from a bleary-eyed Jennifer. The line for Frosted Delights donuts circled through the seating area and down the glass exterior as hungry post-Thanksgiving family members hunted for their next sugary fix. Ariane held Jennifer extra-long in a morning hug before her departure.

"You tell that Mila girl we're all pulling for her," Ariane breathed.

"I'll tell her."

Amelia hovered outside the bakery with Camilla and Olivia already in the vehicle. Jennifer leaped into her now-familiar position in the back-left seat and buckled herself in. None of the other girls looked as though they'd gotten a wink of sleep, either.

"Tell us the truth, Jen. Did you even try to go to bed?" Camilla teased gently.

"I put my head on the pillow for a few minutes," Jennifer confessed. "But there was no way I could just fall asleep before seeing Mila. My body wouldn't calm down. And so, I baked."

Amelia parked the car outside the post-surgery wing of the hospital, where Camilla led them through the double-wide doors with authority. Camilla was accustomed to the multiple smells and sights and sounds the hospital offered, but for Jennifer's palate, each seemed alarming and sinister. Even a strange beep in the distance made her distrustful.

Mila's room was listed as 333. As they turned the corner to reach it, they ran nearly head-first into police officer Liam, whose cheeks sagged with exhaustion. He blinked at them for a moment as though trying to remember who on earth they were.

"She's awake," he told them.

"How does she seem?" Jennifer demanded.

Liam grumbled inwardly. "I don't know. I haven't— um. I haven't gone in. I will after you. After..." He continued to stutter to himself as he marched away.

Jennifer turned to watch as he disappeared around the corner like a lost puppy. Camilla muttered under her breath, "Is that really the kind of guy we want watching over the justice system?" But Amelia scolded her immediately and said, "He's clearly in shock. Who knows what other stuff he's seen over the years?" This left the girls quiet.

Amelia's pregnant belly was the first to enter Room 333, which seemed fitting. Upon her appearance, Mila cooed, which was a welcome sound to Jennifer's ears, even before she saw her completely.

"Oh, Amelia! Are you even bigger than you were last week?" Mila offered sleepily.

Amelia stopped short as the other girls crowded around her, a couple of feet from the length of Mila's bed.

There she was. The head cheerleader. The Edgartown High School Beauty.

Her face seemed to have taken several gashes from shattered glass. There was a bandage over her eyebrow and across her cheek and over the corner of her lip. Her arms and hands were similarly bandaged and her legs, well, Jennifer couldn't bring herself to glance down there, not yet. Her smile remained beautiful, as did her eyes.

"Typical of you to look like a beauty queen even without makeup and after a serious accident," Jennifer lightly teased as she stepped forward to kiss her friend gently on the cheek.

"Yeah, Mila. Give it a rest, won't you?" Olivia's voice cracked as she stepped around to the other side of the white bed and collapsed at the edge of a chair.

Mila's smile waned for a split second. "I just woke up a little while ago. Funny to hear everything from the doctor. He told me a story about myself I hardly remember."

"Dr. Jefferson is a really wonderful surgeon," Camilla returned. "I was relieved when I heard he was in charge of you."

"I'm glad to know the man in charge of my bones was the best one there is," Mila offered, trying on a joke.

The other girls exchanged glances. Nobody knew how to handle this. Nobody knew how to lighten the mood.

"Have you seen Isabelle?" Mila asked, suddenly meek.

"Last night," Jennifer affirmed. "You made me an emergency contact all those years ago."

"Gosh, yes. I forgot I did that," Mila said. "How does she seem?"

Jennifer staggered. "She's fine. A few cuts here and there and a broken arm."

"Broken arm? Gosh." Mila closed her eyes as though the imagined pain of her daughter was much greater than her personal pain.

"She's upset," Jennifer continued. "She blames herself for the accident. She explained that you two were fighting when it happened."

Mila grimaced. "I can hardly remember the conversation right now. My head's still a mess and ringing."

"I called Zane this morning," Amelia told her. "He's on his way back to the island and should arrive within the next hour."

"Oh goodness. How silly," Mila said.

"Darling, it's not silly that your child wants to be with you after you were in a serious car accident," Camilla returned.

"It's nothing major," Mila countered. "My legs are asleep. That's all." She shivered into a strange laugh, coughed, then added, "Oh, you girls don't like my jokes this morning. Did I lose my sense of humor in the accident, along with my ability to walk?"

Her eyes darkened for a split second. Jennifer's stomach felt hollow and cold.

"Honey, we're just so glad you're okay," Jennifer breathed as she stepped closer and slid a hand over Mila's only non-bandaged one.

"We stayed up in the parking lot until we learned the surgery was a success," Olivia whispered.

"And you look like you did, too." Mila tried again with a joke. "What have I told you about getting your beauty sleep? It's the single-most-important element of aging gracefully. I swear, you go unconscious for a few hours, and all hell breaks loose."

This time, all four of the other Sisters of Edgartown did crack into smiles. This was their Mila. She wanted to prove to them that she could be the same, despite the horror of the situation. Everyone was still alive, spirit intact.

Amelia decided to run out to get them a to-go breakfast from the nearby Sunrise Cove Bistro. "Just like you said, Mila, I'm bigger than last week and getting bigger all the time," she said. "Gotta keep this baby fed and we have to get your energy up! Nothing like some surgery to wipe a girl out."

Mila giggled. "Yep. Surgery is up there with spin class. Exhausting!"

"You said it," Amelia quipped as she headed back into the hallway, armed with breakfast orders.

"Guessing my doctor wouldn't be too pleased if I drank a mimosa this morning," Mila shot under her breath.

"Maybe the mantra should be— get-well-first, mimosa-later," Camilla tried.

"Someone in this hospital room is boring, and it's not the girl with no legs," Mila tried.

"Good grief," Olivia said as she burst into laughter. "You're too much."

"Your parents and sisters should be here later this morning," Camilla explained then.

"Oh, great. I can't wait for my mom to come to tell me that if I'd only gone into the medical field, this wouldn't have happened. She's great at shaming you for your biggest mistakes," Mila quipped.

"We can hold a perimeter outside your hospital room, so they keep their distance," Jennifer teased.

"I knew I needed you here, Jennifer Conrad." Mila's eyes glittered strangely, as though with every moment, she struggled not to give herself over to her tears.

About twenty minutes later, the rehabilitation nurse in charge of the next steps in Mila's health journey arrived to speak with Mila. Mila demanded that her girls remain in the hospital room for the conversation.

"They're my family," she explained. "My husband passed away, and I ended up marrying four women to take his place."

"Four?" The nurse counted only three.

"The other's out getting breakfast," Mila affirmed. "No rest for my weary wives."

The rehabilitation nurse introduced herself as Beth Leopold. Jennifer was pretty sure this woman was the fiancé of a member of the Montgomery family, probably Andrew, who'd just returned the previous Christmas after years off the island, including many in the service. When Jennifer asked Beth about her relation to the Montgomery family, Beth blushed and confirmed.

"We're engaged but haven't set a date yet," she explained. "I'm off to see his family this afternoon for Thanksgiving leftovers and Christmas specials. My family's all passed on, and it's such a comfort for me to have a place to go for the holidays. There's so much love between the Sheridan and Montgomery families. Sometimes, that love overwhelms me."

"How beautiful," Olivia swooned.

"It's not a bad family to involve yourself with, that's for sure," Mila said. "Steven was the only Montgomery around our age, and he was swooped up pretty early. You snooze, you lose."

Beth chuckled. "I guess I got lucky with Andy."

After these pleasantries, Beth went on to describe the next several phases of Mila's rehabilitation journey. Beth explained that she'd helped multiple accident victims through similar realms, often with very good results.

"I've seen your chart and am very familiar with your injuries and how we can ease you through them once your bones properly bond back together. It's about working with your body rather than against it and growing stronger with each passing day. Obviously, when you return home in a few days, you'll have a wheelchair, which will take some getting used to."

At this, all the color drained from Mila's cheeks. It seemed she hadn't actually considered that her life might look a whole lot different outside the hospital walls.

"A wheelchair?"

"You'll get accustomed to it quickly," Beth explained.

"I live alone," Mila countered as her fear mounted.

"You won't anymore," Camilla quipped.

Mila's eyes widened as silence fell around them. "No. It's too much to ask of you girls."

"Are you kidding?" Jennifer returned. "What else are we good for? We're not just friends to approve lipstick color."

Mila's bottom lip curled out as she considered this.

"I can also ask Liam for help," she offered. "So it wouldn't have to go only on your shoulders."

Suddenly, there was a rustling at the door as Amelia entered, carrying several plastic bags of what seemed to be enough food to feed a small army. She stopped short at the sight of Beth Leopold.

"Guess what, Amelia? I'm going to be in a wheelchair," Mila blurted out from her bed.

Amelia positioned the bags of food on the side table. "Sounds like we're all moving into Mila's?"

Mila's face broke into a vibrant smile, maybe the biggest Jennifer had seen since their arrival.

"I guess I always wanted servants," Mila teased after a long pause. "Finally, I get my chance!"

"Oh, great. She's already ahead of herself," Jennifer teased.

Beth finished up her speech and prepared to depart to allow the girls to eat their breakfast together. When she stepped into the hallway, Jennifer, guided by some unknown force, followed after her.

"Beth?"

Beth turned back to catch Jennifer's gaze. "Yes, how can I help you?"

"You really think um. Do you really believe she'll..." Jennifer lost her train of thought as her cheeks sagged.

"Do I really believe she'll walk again?" Beth asked.

"Yes."

Beth sucked in a deep breath before answering. "I have seen patients like Mila eventually walk again, yes. It will be a long and difficult road. Honestly, based on what I read about the accident, Mila is very lucky to be alive. I think you five should focus on that this morning. Focus on the love between you rather than what has potentially been lost. Mila seems in good spirits. Make sure you keep her there as best as you can. It's a mental game from here on out, but she can do this if she puts her mind to it."

Jennifer thanked Beth before Beth turned on her white nurse's shoes and squeaked out of sight. Toward the far end of the hallway, Liam remained leaning against the wall, as though he gave himself a never-ending pep talk as a way to enter Mila's room. *What scared him so much?*

But Mila didn't need Liam, not then. She needed her sisters. She needed funny conversation and proof that there was still so much to live for. Jennifer drew her eyes away from Liam and returned to the room, which already spun with laughter and love. It was enough.

Chapter Seven

The girls hung around the hospital all throughout the day. As Mila's parents had arrived that morning from Europe already, having taken an immediate flight back, they rushed to her side the moment they could— bringing with them a host of their own worries and anxiety. Mila took a much-needed nap after her parents departed, calling their visit, *"Just another car crash."* Isabelle was released from her hospital room around lunchtime, which allowed her to rush into her mother's room to declare that she would finish out "at least this school year" before she headed off to model in New York City. To this, Mila just laughed and said, "Honey, you should follow your dreams. Life's too short for anything else."

Jennifer was in a text conversation with her loved ones, who wanted constant updates about both Mila's health and Jennifer's mental health. Jennifer wanted to scold them about their worry for her. She wasn't the one in the hospital bed. She wasn't the one who'd nearly lost her life. Even still, their care was a necessary boost.

Back in the waiting room, Amelia drew out her computer, which she seemed to always have on hand, and began to craft a schedule to ensure Mila was never left alone.

"We should work that out later," Olivia tried. "It's too soon to know how it should go."

"Just let her make a spreadsheet," Jennifer returned with a wry laugh. "It's her happy place."

Amelia cast them a sharp glance. "I just want Mila to know she'll be taken care of. Especially since Liam seems to be, well, not the most reliable."

"I saw him running around the halls earlier. Still no sign that he stepped in to say hi," Jennifer said softly.

But when they returned after Mila's nap, they found Liam seated beside her, holding her hand loosely as he spoke to her in tender tones. Mila's smile had fallen from her face completely, as though Liam's anxiety-riddled behavior had echoed back through her.

"I've seen it time and again. Angry drivers at the wheel. Unsure of their surroundings," Liam continued.

"I understand, but the accident already happened. You can't talk me out of it at this point," Mila countered, almost angrily.

The other girls froze in the doorway. Mila sensed their presence, turned, and greeted them with a lukewarm smile.

"Hi, Liam," Jennifer greeted. "Good to see you." She implied her anger with the adverb, "finally."

Liam glanced toward the ground. He shuffled to his feet as the girls gathered on the opposite side of the bed. "Guess I'll go grab myself another cup of coffee. You girls need anything?"

"No, thank you. We're good," Amelia replied darkly as Liam rose and headed for the door.

They listened as he took off down the hallway. Mila blew the air out of her lips.

"Men are sometimes so fragile, aren't they?" she finally offered. "Peter was like that sometimes if the kids got injured. It was like the world ended. I just grabbed a band-aide and sent them back outside."

"You know women are heartier than men," Camilla countered. "I mean, we give birth for crying out loud. Blood doesn't scare us, either. We have to live with all of it. The messy bits of life."

"Don't talk about giving birth," Amelia touted. "I'm in the denial stage."

"He'll come around," Olivia affirmed regarding Liam. "He's just freaked after his years on the force. I'm sure he never imagined something like this could happen to someone he loves."

Mila shifted slightly beneath her overly thin white blankets. "Our relationship is still so new. It could even still be called a fling, you know? I'm sure he didn't reckon for something like this. It's a lot of pressure. We went from wine nights and silly dates to... a wheelchair?"

The other girls exchanged worried glances. Mila spoke a truth they couldn't dispute. Even still, they wanted to expect more from a man who supposedly "loved" or at least "really liked" Mila. She deserved the world.

"I guess it'll take getting used to for everyone," Mila tried then. "And we'll just see where the chips fall."

When visiting hours finished for the day, Amelia drove them all back to where they belonged. Jennifer hopped into her car outside the Frosted Delights Bakery and stared into space for a full five minutes before she started the engine. Her mind had hit its top bandwidth. Thoughts had lost their meaning.

When she reached the home she now shared with Derek, she discovered another three vehicles parked outside: Nick's, her parents, and Emma's. Jennifer hadn't envisioned anything but Derek alone in front of the television.

Inside, Derek stepped out from the living room with a, "Welcome home, honey!" He kissed her gently on the lips and swept a hand across the small of her back as he guided her into a Christmas-Wonderland of a brand-new, freshly-cut Christmas tree, a platter of Christmas cookies, Christmas music spilling from the speaker, and some of the people she loved the most— Nick, Stacy, Emma, Emma's husband, Will, along with her parents, John and Ariane Conrad. Jennifer found herself tossed from hug to hug as everyone gave her their condolences.

"I had no idea you two were coming in," she said to one set of newlyweds, Emma and Will.

"Dad begged us to," Emma teased. "So sentimental."

Jennifer knew that Derek and Emma had lost Emma's mother around Christmas, which made them extra-nostalgic around this time of year. All she could do was offer love and support for their memories. Sometimes, memories were all you had.

Emma and Stacy had put together a beautifully roasted chicken with savory vegetables and freshly-baked rolls. Someone poured Jennifer a glass of wine while Ariane had a general freak-out about Stacy's pregnancy.

"A great-grandmother! Jennifer, did you hear that?"

"I sure did, Mom," Jennifer offered, making eye contact with Nick, who gave her a funny face.

"And we hardly had to wait after the wedding!" Ariane continued.

"That's what my mom said," Stacy affirmed. "She keeps thanking us. I'm like, well, it was an accident. But you're welcome?" She giggled and placed her head tenderly on Nick's chest. They were the perfect portrait of a newly married couple.

"Don't get any ideas about us, Dad," Emma warned as they sat around the dining room table. "We've got a lot of plans before all that."

"She wants to drag me around the world," Will admitted, feigning annoyance. "Japan. Vietnam. Hawaii. Can you believe it? All I want to do is sit on the couch and watch my life go by."

Emma rolled her eyes playfully as she tore open her freshly-baked roll. Ariane commented that Emma had a real knack for baking, to which Emma returned, "My mother taught me the recipe. I always bring it around this time of year. It helps me remember her better."

Jennifer's eyes met Derek's over the table. His eyes shimmered for a split second before he returned his attention to his food. How strange that they sat at the table, surrounded by ghosts. Perhaps that's what Christmas was all about.

Ariane pestered Jennifer for more information regarding Mila's health. Jennifer confessed that it would be a "very long road" and that Amelia already had a spreadsheet cooked up for how the girls would help out.

"That's no surprise," Ariane affirmed. "Whenever you girls got into any kind of trouble, the other five of you were there to pick up the pieces." Her face grew clouded as she added, "Well, the other five of you when Michelle was around. Such a funny bunch, the six of you, were. I still love that old photograph that hangs in the bakery." She then glanced toward Emma, who was a relatively new audience for her old stories and added, "They went everywhere together— they were attached at the hip. I couldn't have imagined at the time that any of them would actually grow up." She then turned to catch Stacy's eyes to add, "You're about to encounter all that emotion and more. Motherhood! What a gift it was and still is. Goodness, I should really give Mila's mother a call."

Jennifer explained that Mila's parents had taken a direct flight back from Europe and arrived just in time to exhaust Mila into a nap.

"What do you mean?" Ariane demanded. "Why would they exhaust her?"

Jennifer had to suppress a smile. It was typical of parents not to understand the little, intricate ways they drove their children nuts. She assumed she, too, had her little ways with Nick. Stacy and Nick's baby would find their nuanced annoyances with their parents, too. It was just the generational divide.

After dinner, everyone gathered around a selection of boxes of Christmas ornaments in the living room. Stacy put on Michael Buble's Christmas CD and hummed in time to the music as she twirled into Nick. Jennifer straddled herself between several boxes, many of which she'd moved over from her and Joel's old house. Emma had brought several boxes herself, ornaments she hadn't chosen for her and Will's tree, but ones that had previously hung on her childhood trees.

With Jennifer and Derek's boxes together, it was like looking at a hodgepodge of decades of Christmas memories from alternate timelines. Somehow, they'd made their way here together and would soon hang on a brand-new Christmas tree to mark time through another holiday.

"This was your grandmother's gift to your mom and me after you were born," Derek said to Emma as he lifted a little pair of silver shoes from their Christmas ornament box and dangled them upon a branch. "You were such a tiny thing! The shoes could have fit you back then."

Emma's cheeks flushed crimson as she gazed at the bobbing pair of shoes on the tree, which had the year 1998 engraved across the base. The year Emma had been born.

"Hard to believe we're around adults born in the late nineties," Ariane offered from the comfort of the corner chair. "They were just little babies at the turn of the century."

This led to a funny conversation about Derek's fears around Y2K when everyone thought the country would darken and all data would be lost.

"After many years of hard work, my business was finally growing. I had a young toddler at home. We'd just gotten a new apartment. I was seriously freaked out, to say the least," he explained as he stretched tinsel across the tree. "My wife teased me to no end about it and, of course, had a field day when the clock struck midnight and nothing happened."

Emma giggled. "I can just imagine Mom teasing you. She was always like that."

"Yeah, yeah. I was a little high-strung," Derek offered as he rolled his eyes.

"Joel and I didn't have many pennies to rub together at the time," Jennifer said with a laugh, grateful to swap stories from this singular time. "We had baby Nick, a tiny house, and our dreams. I guess if the world had gone dark, we'd have started a farm and lived off the land."

"Jen, honey, you've killed every plant I've given you," Ariane returned.

Jennifer giggled. She grabbed the half-drunk bottle of wine from the coffee table and walked around to deliver refills. She remembered what Beth Leopold had said earlier that day about the comfort of family and how she'd only just discovered it with her fiancé's. How remarkable that Jennifer had that in spades.

With the Christmas tree decorated and the stockings hung, the Thatcher and Conrad families nibbled Christmas cookies, sipped wine, swapped stories, and watched as the fire roared in the fireplace. Jennifer grew quiet as her father explained a rather complicated story that involved people nobody in the room had ever met nor heard of. She lifted her phone to find a single text from Mila — not to the group, but only to Jennifer.

MILA: I'm trying my darnedest to be grateful for what I have.

MILA: But damn. I had some nice legs.

MILA: It will be sad to see them go.

Jennifer's eyes filled with tears. She closed them briefly as she drummed up some kind of response. Derek's hand cupped her knee tenderly as he noticed her swirling.

JENNIFER: No offense, but as your best friend, I always loved your smile more than your legs. Let's keep your smile going. Love you forever.

Chapter Eight

It was a difficult thing to wake up at the time you wanted to when your body ached for more sleep. Mila's eyelids slowly widened to reveal a blistering white room around her as a machine-marked time on her heartbeat directly beside her, like a nagging robot. A familiar voice mumbled something before directing all attention toward Mila.

"Mom! You're awake."

That term: Mom. It dragged Mila's psyche out of the depths and back on planet Earth. As her neck still felt terribly stiff, she peeked her eyes rightward to catch Isabelle, all bundled up in her father's college sweatshirt and a pair of flannel pajama pants. She wore no makeup, and her hair was greased slightly, just some strings hanging near her eyes. Behind her stood her brother, Zane, who'd arrived back from college the afternoon before.

"Did you kids have a party at the house last night?" Mila asked in a sneaky tone.

Isabelle's jaw dropped. "Mom! We would never."

Mila tried to laugh just as her stomach tensed and spasmed with pain. "That was always your thing. Don't gaslight me into thinking it wasn't."

Zane rolled his eyes and stepped around to sit at the edge of her bed. Once there, he took her hand. God, he was handsome, the spitting-image of Peter at his age. Mila hadn't met Peter till he'd been in his forties, still a jaw-droppingly handsome man.

"We're grown up now, Mom," Zane articulated.

"Oh right. I forgot," Mila teased.

Zane and Isabelle exchanged glances. Mila struggled to remember what day it was. *Sunday, probably?* The accident had happened on Black Friday. Yesterday had been a blur of conversation and stress from her parents, who'd been flustered after their quick trek back over the ocean from their planned adventure through Europe. When Mila had suggested they shouldn't have come home, they'd spat with silly anger.

"We were thinking," Isabelle began.

"Uh oh," Mila tried. Bit by bit, she felt more engaged with the world.

"That we might want to do our classes online the next few weeks so we can stay home and take care of you," Zane finished.

"No. No way." Mila's eyes widened. "I won't be the reason you miss classes. I'm willing to bet you've already missed your fair share over the semester."

Zane grumbled inwardly. "We're allowed to miss three per class..."

"There we go," Mila quipped.

"Mom, seriously. We'll be all freaked out about you if we're off the island," Isabelle admitted. Her right hand shifted over her left arm, which was armed with a cast.

Something strange and cold shifted into Mila's belly. She'd done this to her baby. What did she care, truly, about her own body? The small gashes across Isabelle's face were additional reminders of how foolish she'd been. The previous afternoon, when Liam had visited, he'd told her over and over just how safe she should have been. She couldn't take it back. Guilt enveloped her.

"Mom?" Zane waved a hand to catch her eyes. "You still there?"

"I'm here." Mila closed and reopened her eyes. Focus. She needed to focus. "I just don't think it's necessary that you two stick around. You should head back to your dorms. This afternoon, even. I have my girls and I have Liam."

Did she have Liam, though? He'd looked at her with eyes like voids.

"I love you," Mila said, her voice firm. It was her mother's voice. "And all I would do if you stayed here is worry that your education was falling apart because of my stupid injury. I do not want this to impact our lives any more than it already has to. Is that clear?"

Isabelle and Zane left to catch the two p.m. ferry. Their departure sent shatters through Mila's heart. Again, in the silence of herself, she tried to "feel" her legs, but as far as her mind was concerned, her body ended halfway down her thighs.

It was a remarkable and eerie development. It terrified her to death.

Around two, Liam appeared in his police officer uniform, something Mila had previously thought to be ridiculously handsome. He greeted her with a cold kiss on the cheek and sat in the same chair Isabelle had sat in. He looked strangely defeated.

"I'm sorry about this," Mila finally offered, not knowing why she'd just apologized.

Liam tried to find a smile. "Your girls are down the hall. I asked them to give me a few minutes with you."

"What can I say? When you're this famous, you always have a posse," Mila countered.

Liam coughed into laughter. "Did you get some sleep last night?"

"I did. Weird dreams, though. Not that I want to be your crazy girlfriend who tells you her dreams," Mila returned. "Nobody wants to hear them."

Liam gently splayed his hand over hers upon the white sheet. The robot gave a resounding beep, a reminder that she remained alive.

"I hate that I have a shift today. I tried to take the day off, but you know— the holidays and all that jazz. It's such a busy time."

"Busy is right," Mila echoed.

Her legs had created a strange rift between them. She could visualize the next steps just as well as he could: him, wheeling her around in a wheelchair as they tried to handle "date night." Him: helping her into a bathtub so she could wash herself. Him: picking her up and splaying her into the bed they'd once frequently shared. How would sex work? How would they continue to build their fledgling relationship?

Had they already lost something she'd thought was rather beautiful?

"Anyway. I'll send the girls in, now," Liam said as he shot to his feet.

"I know you didn't ask for this," Mila offered.

Liam stopped short as his arms hung sadly at his sides. "Nobody asks for a lot of the bad things that happen. I've seen them time and time again."

Mila gave a half-shrug. "But this isn't everyone else. This is us."

Liam scrubbed a hand over his forehead. "I have to go." He then turned and headed down the hallway, leaving Mila in the silence of herself and really unsure of what would happen next.

With just about an hour left of visiting time, a familiar woman appeared in the doorway of Mila's hospital room. She was sixty-four-year-old Hannah Arlington, a recently hired employee at Mila's esthetician salon. Mila had been mesmerized with Hannah's beauty secrets, which had led to a conversation about Hannah's actual age versus the age she looked. "You don't look a day over fifty," Mila had breathed at the time. "You have to bring your magic to the salon. The women of the Vineyard need you."

Hannah carried a bouquet of pink lilies and wore a periwinkle winter coat and a pair of heels. Her styled-sterling-white hair curled around her ears delicately, and her bright blue eyes twinkled as she peered out at the five women before her. At sixty-four, she brought an earnestness and timidity of a much younger woman.

"Hannah!" Mila cried. "I didn't expect you."

Hannah bowed her head gingerly and gestured with the flowers. "I couldn't handle just sitting around the house and thinking about you. I wanted to come to see you for myself."

"That's so sweet of you. Girls, this is my newer employee at the salon, Hannah. Hannah, these are my best friends, Olivia, Amelia, Jennifer, and Camilla."

Hannah greeted them with soft words as she splayed the lilies across a table that had already been stuffed to the gills with other bouquets. Silence stretched between the six of them, so much so that Mila asked for a few minutes alone with Hannah to "catch up."

One by one, the women Mila loved the most stepped out of the hospital room, which allowed Hannah the seat closest to Mila. In the strange silence that followed, Mila realized that she knew very little about her newest employee, save the fact that she had one of the best skincare regimes she'd ever heard of.

"It's so sweet of you to come by," Mila tried again.

Hannah blushed. "I'm sure it's silly. You've got your family and your beautiful friends. I just wanted to come to tell you how much you've meant to me over the past few months. The job really saved me during a dark time. And I wanted you to know that, well, I'm happy to pick up extra shifts now that you won't be able to work for a while."

"Thank you, Hannah. Really." Mila swallowed as she hunted for something else to say. "How was your Thanksgiving?"

Hannah's nostrils flared the slightest bit. "Oh, just about as quiet as every other year. I don't like to make a big fuss."

"What about your family? Don't they drag you into one celebration or another?"

Hannah's lips parted in surprise. "I don't have much in the way of family these days. My parents passed on, as you can imagine, and my sister lives in California. She sends me the most beautiful postcards, but I always tell her, there's no life for me off the Vineyard."

Mila's heart felt bruised. What good was looking any way at all, of having any beautiful skin routine, of fighting to fit in with the world of fashion if you had no love to call your own?

"You should have told me you didn't have plans," Mila said softly. "You would have been very welcome with my family. My mother can be a real piece of work, and my sisters are know-it-alls, but otherwise, we have a pretty good time."

"And your twins. They must have been around, too," Hannah tried.

Mila's guilt deepened. It was clear this woman knew a great deal more about her than she did about Hannah. She'd been nothing but a dutiful worker over the past few months. Why hadn't Mila allowed herself to be curious about her? She knew a great deal about her other employees, mostly because they gabbed and gossiped endlessly about their boyfriends, husbands, and potential dates.

Probably that Sunday evening, Hannah had looked around her empty house and reasoned— *well, Mila is one of the only people I know. Why not pay her a visit?*

"It's so wonderful to see you," Mila tried again, as though they could have a proper conversation without any background information. "You always give me hope for fashion over sixty."

Hannah chuckled kindly. "I always longed to be an artist. I found that my artistic eye is better used through clothing. Although to be honest with you, I recently set up a little painting studio in my house. Silly, maybe, to start painting at my age, but how else should I spend my time?"

Mila was accustomed to the same-old stories with the same-old people she had loved her entire life. Here was a woman who was hardly heard. And here Mila was: in a hospital bed, unclear about the rest of her life, yet eager to listen.

"Why don't you tell me more about yourself, Hannah? I'd really love to know," Mila whispered. "I can't promise I'll stay awake much longer. The medicine they have me on knocks me out cold. But I'd love to hear a story if you're willing to tell it."

Hannah's eyes shone with excitement as she dove through the first story, which involved her and her sister's wild cross-country drive from the Vineyard all the way to her sister's new home in California. Sometime between a bad mechanic job in Oklahoma and a handsome motorcyclist in Nevada, Mila crept into the darkness of sleep. Hannah's voice was a welcome relief. It guided her toward comfort.

Chapter Nine

Five days. It had been five days since the accident. It seemed ridiculous to remember this, as it seemed time lacked any kind of meaning. Even still, as time passed, they moved toward some sort of betterment in Mila's condition. Time forward meant time away from the worst of it all. It meant time to heal.

It was the afternoon, a Wednesday. Jennifer hurriedly typed a memo for her social media firm assistant, a chirpy blonde named Samantha, and rushed from the second floor of the downtown office building, headed for her car. As Oliver remained out of town till Saturday morning, Jennifer had pledged herself as Amelia's right-hand partner for all things baby. Amelia happened to have an appointment in no less than twenty minutes, which made Jennifer about six minutes late.

Amelia hovered in the foyer of the downtown government office building, all bundled up in a bulbous winter coat and a dark green scarf. Jennifer swept toward the curb nearest the door as

Amelia popped out and delivered a sterling grin. Ordinarily, Amelia might have said something cutting, like, *"I thought you weren't going to make it."* But as she slid into Jennifer's front passenger seat, she greeted her brightly. "Thank you so much for doing this. It means to world to me."

"Ugh, you don't have to do that. I know I was late."

Amelia waved her hand through the air flippantly. "Come on, Jen. All I can do this week is feel grateful for Mila's successful surgery and my overall healthy baby. At forty-one! What more could I possibly want?"

"Maybe your best friend to arrive when she said she would?" Jennifer teased as she moved the car back out onto the road.

"Life's about compromise," Amelia teased right back. "I take you as you are— lateness and all."

The gynecologist's office needed an update. It seemed almost exactly the same as it had back when Jennifer had been pregnant with Nick, around the time of her graduation from high school in 1998. The paintings that hung crooked on every wall echoed a very different modern art aesthetic, something incredibly retro and incredibly ugly (in Jennifer's modest opinion), and even the music that spat out of the speakers very, very quietly was soft rock from the late seventies.

"It's good to know that not everything changes so much," she whispered to Amelia, who giggled in return.

"I know. It feels peaceful to hear Crosby, Stills, Nash, and Young— a band my dad loved so much, while I sit here in fear about having my first baby," Amelia returned softly. "Makes me feel like maybe my baby will still be able to see some of the world I grew to love, too. Maybe the old isn't so lost, even with non-stop changes."

Amelia was called a few minutes later. "See? We're right on time," Amelia said as they headed for the doctor's office. "We would have waited on those sticky chairs for another ten minutes if you'd been on time."

Jennifer blushed. "I guess there's a method to my madness."

Once inside the office itself, Amelia slung herself back on the chair with two stirrups. Just as she had with Nick, Jennifer held her breath as the technician squelched clear gel across Amelia's lower belly. In a moment, Amelia's baby appeared on the monitor— a prominent head and a curved spine with little legs and arms. Jennifer still couldn't breathe. She imagined Nick seeing this view of his little one incredibly soon— imagined the wide-open, scary feeling he would encounter when he first witnessed his baby's birth. It was one thing to experience life events; it was another to watch your baby experience it himself.

"Everything looks great," the technician explained to Amelia. "The heartbeat is normal and healthy. You're about seven months, which means I'm sure that you have a birth plan set up."

Jennifer snorted. Amelia cast her a rueful glance.

"What? Did I miss something?" the technician asked.

"It's just that my friends think I have a planning problem," Amelia informed her.

"Never a bad thing when it comes to having a baby," the technician explained. "However, I have to assure you. Your due date is just an approximation. Your baby will come when your baby wants to come."

"Oh no," Amelia said, mocking herself with bulged eyes. "Jennifer... How will I make a spreadsheet for a baby who doesn't know what she or he wants?"

Jennifer laughed outright. "And this is only the beginning. Imagine, Amelia, if your baby happens to be... Type B?"

Amelia gasped as the technician burst into laughter of her own.

"All right, all right. Let's get back to business," she stated, grinning ear-to-ear.

Back in Jennifer's car, they received a message from the Sister Group Chat.

CAMILLA: Come by the house? Andrea's having a last-minute bride-meltdown and I have to say, I need backup.

"We can swing over and then head up to the hospital?" Jennifer glanced toward Amelia to confirm.

"Of course. It sounded like Mila had another few visitors today. Her sisters stopped by to ruin her life, followed by her mother."

"Oh great," Jennifer returned sarcastically. "We'll go save her soon."

When they reached Camilla's, they sat in rapt attention as Andrea, Charlotte, and Camilla confirmed the last elements of the weekend's wedding. When Andrea went into an emotional tizzy—a sort of, "Oh gosh, it's all going to be a disaster, isn't it? Why did I think I wanted such a big wedding?" Camilla also found herself faltering. This left Amelia and Jennifer to pick up the pieces, while ultimately, Charlotte made the final decision. It was kind of a failed assembly line of emotional baggage.

An hour after their arrival, Andrea swooned and cast herself across the couch. Camilla rushed to her side, her cheeks blotchy, and demanded when she had last eaten. This left Jennifer and Amelia in the kitchen, chopping up vegetables for a low-carb, high-nutrient salad, the only sort of thing Andrea would put in her mouth before the big day. Amelia snuck a carrot between her teeth and said, "If me and Oliver ever get married, I think we'll just go to city hall. I've felt all this residual stress from both Nick and Andrea's wedding, and I've had enough."

"Things have really changed since we did our little weddings back in the day," Jennifer agreed. "Stacy wanted the kind of wedding you find in Home and Garden, and Andrea has a very particular eye."

"Well, she does go to fashion school in the city," Amelia countered. "I guess she's allowed."

"I, for one, can't wait for Christmas." This was Camilla, who stepped into the kitchen, pulled open the fridge, and drew out a bottle of Chardonnay. She filled her wine glass and sipped nearly half of it before she offered the wine to Jennifer, Charlotte, and Andrea.

"No offense, Jen, but I shouldn't have to offer. You know how to open my fridge," she teased.

Jonathon breezed in and out after that, grabbing a slice of red pepper along the way. His work remained hyper-focused on Oliver's development project on the northern edge of the island, where he worked as the head of construction. He kissed both Andrea and Camilla on the cheek, then muttered to Jennifer, "I told Andrea I would pay her to elope, but she wouldn't go for it."

Jennifer giggled. "Oh, you. You're a big sap. You're going to love walking her down the aisle."

Jonathon dipped his head from left to right. "I know, I know. I'll be the blubbering one on the dance floor."

When they finally sat Andrea down with a huge salad and a small slice of buttered bread, Jennifer and Amelia headed back to Jen's car to meet Olivia up at the hospital. Camilla reported she'd be there later, as she had an all-night nursing shift anyway.

"Just when I think we're done with all the minutia of this wedding, another thing crops up," she grumbled as Jennifer and Amelia donned their coats. "It better be the best day of all of our lives."

Mila did have a visitor up at the hospital: the woman in her sixties who worked at the esthetician salon and seemed to have incredibly inventive and chic outfits, the likes of which had made the other sisters gush "I hope to be like that when I'm sixty-four."

From outside Mila's room, it appeared that Hannah and Mila were in the midst of an intense conversation. Hannah furrowed her brow as she spread her fingers wide to articulate something. The light flashed across her vintage rings beautifully.

"What do you think they're talking about?" Amelia breathed.

"No idea." Jennifer reached up and clacked her knuckles across the wood.

From within, there came a small cry. "Come in!"

As the door swung open, Hannah erupted from her chair and began to gather her things.

"You don't have to rush out," Jennifer said brightly.

"There's plenty of space. We just came to pester our girl," Amelia returned.

Hannah seemed flustered. "Oh, don't mind me. I just stopped by on my way home from the salon to update Mila on what's what."

"So helpful, Hannah. Thank you," Mila said.

"You're looking brighter today." Jennifer beamed as she eased herself directly onto the chair Hannah had vacated.

"Hannah brought me some of her skin creams. She's trying to help me age backward."

"As if you'd need my help with that," Hannah said from the door. "Good evening, Miss Mila. I'll see you soon. And I'll bring those chocolates I told you about. I have a hunch you'll love them."

Once the door clipped shut behind Hannah, the air shifted toward something Jennifer understood— a world of just the girls she loved the most. Very soon, Olivia would arrive, and after that, Camilla would check-in before her shift. Day-by-day, they pushed forward through territory they couldn't fully understand.

"Hannah's been such a dear," Mila said as she adjusted herself on her pillow. "I never knew much about her, but she has fascinating stories. It's just one after the other with her. It's like watching a TV show better than anything on TV right now."

"And you didn't have any idea about her past?" Jennifer asked.

"No. And I wonder why she offers it up now? She's always seemed so timid and far away. I learned she doesn't have much family."

"Maybe she thinks of you as more of her family since you work together every day," Amelia offered. "When I was single and working with the same people all the time, I think I thought of them differently than they thought of me. They had husbands and wives and children to get back to. I had you girls, but besides that, they were my work family."

"I'm sure you're right." Mila tucked a strand of hair behind her ear, then continued. "In any case, with all the strain between my mother and me, it's kind of nice to have a friend in an older woman like Hannah. Especially one who seems so..." She trailed off as she considered the words. "I don't know. I'll probably end up a whole lot like her, to be honest with you."

"Don't you dare say that," Jennifer blared. "You know we'll move in with you the minute you try to take up some kind of loner mentality."

"That's right. You'll have to help me raise this baby," Amelia teased.

Mila rolled her eyes back. She paused for a long moment before she added, "I can really feel Liam pulling away. For all my upbeat attitude, for all my gratefulness, I can't help but think about my weird year of dating and how I thought all that was over for me. I thought I'd really found someone— someone stable. And now..."

Jennifer drew a hand over Mila's. "I'm sure he's scared. He doesn't know how to do any of this."

Mila's lips curved into a soft smile. "Yeah, but neither do any of you. Not really. But you're showing up for me, every day, despite everything." She paused as tears welled in her eyes. "Thank you for that, really. I don't even know how to express how much it means to me."

Chapter Ten

Mila had grown overly tired of the silly ghost-like hospital gown. After thirty-plus years of fashion obsession, it was borderline humiliating to live out nearly a week of her life in a large cloth bag, greeting guest after guest and trying her darnedest to feel like the Mila they knew and loved.

Well, most of them loved her. After so many whispered words of the like over the previous months, Liam had seemingly backed up on his original idea of them as a couple. She hadn't seen him in three days. She knew because each morning, as she took in the reflection of her gash-filled face in the small hand mirror Jennifer had brought her, she slipped makeup over her lips and smeared eye cream beneath her eyes and counted out the days to herself. "Two days since he was here." "Now, three." It seemed she marked time till their relationship's untimely death.

How funny to lose so much at once— including your ability to walk.

Including your general optimism when it came to the world.

No. She couldn't lean too heavily into that outlook. She knew it would eat up everything else going on in her head.

It was now Thursday. Six days since the accident had happened, and the pain had receded bit by bit. She had grown accustomed to the medication, at least partially, and had now found the strength to sit upright in her hospital bed for the majority of the day, minus the hour or two she sat in her wheelchair as "practice" for the weekend ahead. There was no way in hell she would miss Andrea's big day. She would move mountains to be there— to eat the yummy food and laugh with her sisters and watch Andrea dance her first dance with her beloved man. She so wanted, for just a moment, to pretend that everything was all right.

The in-hospital psychologist arrived at ten sharp that morning. It had already been explained to Mila the necessity of a consultation with the psychologist, as she'd been through such a traumatic event. Mila had always resisted the idea of therapy, as she'd always been of the opinion that a good attitude and enough humor could get you through anything.

As the days passed since the accident, however, her sense of humor and her ability to laugh had almost nearly dried up. This discouraged her even more. It was like she didn't even have herself to lean on any longer.

Mila tried her best to describe this sensation to the psychologist, who was a fifty-something broad-shouldered woman with a remarkably pronounced set of eyebrows— the likes of which Mila might have tweezed a bit if she'd had her in her salon chair.

"You're saying that you feel a sense of loss," the psychologist said now.

"That's right, and it's not even just my legs. It's something else — my optimism, maybe. It's like if everything culminated to this moment of the accident... will anything good even happen after this? I don't know. I feel a bit of jealousy, also, for my best friends, my sisters, who are allowed to keep living the lives they planned to live..." Mila pressed her lips together, frightened of her own dark emotions.

The psychologist nodded firmly. "These are natural things to feel. Your life has been sidelined for the foreseeable future. It will take a mountain of energy to move past this stage and keep going."

Mila's eyes welled with tears, which she refused to let fall. "I feel like those people who used to wait out on the Bridge of Sighs as their whaler husbands and boyfriends left the island for up to five years at a time. I feel that everyone's moving on without me. And I'll just be wheeling along behind them..."

"It's been suggested to me by your doctor that you have a rather good chance to walk again," the psychologist countered. "It's not one hundred percent, as you know. But statistics show that if you focus on the positives of something, you have a higher chance of achieving a positive outcome. If you dwell in these very real, very honest feelings, you could create a darkness within you— one that could disallow you from overcoming your challenges and learning to walk again."

Mila had to wince at this expression, "learn to walk." It reminded her of her twins as they had hobbled across the carpet, with both Peter and Mila staggering behind them, careful to catch them before they fell. When they did, their howling was proof of their fear rather than of their pain. Peter and Mila had known this. Even still, it had made their hearts ache to hear it.

"I've spoken with a number of other patients in similar situations," the psychologist continued.

"Did any of them use their legs again?" Mila breathed.

"Many of them did. Yes."

Mila's heart fluttered like a butterfly.

"And they told me, as they went through the process, that it was better not to put pressure on themselves to return to their old life. They told me they found more beauty in the day-to-day experiences."

"And what about their personal relationships? Did they return to what they'd been before?" Mila didn't want to speak overtly about her police officer boyfriend, as it seemed almost too pathetic.

"Yes and no," the psychologist offered. "But ask yourself this. Do any of your relationships stay the same, ultimately? Or do they find new ways to shift and grow and change as time goes by?"

"Of course, things change," Mila protested, looking at the doc with wide eyes. "But it's not usually so abrupt."

"I believe that things always fall the way they're meant to fall," the psychologist returned. "If someone leaves you as a result of your injuries, you're better off without them. I truly believe that. They're showing you something about themselves— something you're bound never to forget."

It was the fourth day since Mila last saw Liam in the flesh, and it was also the day Jennifer, Amelia, Camilla, and Olivia gathered around her wheelchair and fought over who had the privilege of pushing her out into the gleaming December sun. It was finally time for Mila to take on her life at home— finally, time for her to remove the silly hospital gown and find something a bit more tasteful to wear as her legs healed. It was finally time for her to push beyond the limitations of the previous week and discover where her true boundaries lay.

She certainly wouldn't miss the hospital food, either.

Ultimately, Jennifer wrapped her hands around the wheelchair handles and pushed Mila down the hallway of the hospital. Mila's eyes ate up every scene they passed by: small glances into other hospital rooms, other patients in wheelchairs, nurses shuffling about, children scrambling away from their parents. *What on earth did they think of her?* There in the hospital, it was much more common to see a woman like Mila in a wheelchair. Even still, eyes caught onto hers with curiosity. *What had happened to her? Would she ever walk again?* These questions seemed to burn from the back of their eyes.

Once in the foyer of the hospital, Jennifer wrapped Mila up in a brand-new Chanel scarf, which she and the girls had purchased for Mila as a going home present. Mila adjusted a winter hat on her head and shifted forward just the slightest bit to allow Camilla to strain her winter coat over her arms.

"Let's take a picture!" Olivia cried now.

"To commemorate what exactly? The day I couldn't get my coat on by myself?" Mila tried the joke.

Olivia's face fell. Mila finally mumbled, "All right, Liv. We can do it. Just don't post it anywhere, okay?"

"It's just for us," Olivia murmured. "It's always just for us."

Camilla nabbed a passing nurse to take a photo. As the four others arranged themselves around Mila's wheelchair, flipped their hair, and eased their heads toward Mila's, Mila burned with embarrassment. She wanted no record of herself in a wheelchair.

"Oh, it's perfect," Olivia breathed as she glanced at her phone screen immediately after. "Mila, as usual, you're still our beauty queen."

Still? Mila's cheeks flushed with heat. Back in high school, the fact that Mila had turned heads with such success had been something of a joke. Now, it haunted her. She would certainly turn heads from the wheelchair, but they weren't the sort of heads she wanted.

And Liam had clearly disappeared from her life.

Jennifer and Camilla lifted Mila from the wheelchair and splayed her in the backseat of Jennifer's car. As Mila stared at the car ceiling above her, Olivia and Amelia squabbled over how to disassemble the wheelchair so that it could be placed easily in the back trunk. Finally, Camilla jumped forward and performed the task in two seconds flat.

"Guess we should have asked the nurse in the first place," Amelia breathed.

All the girls had come from separate locations for Mila's departure, which meant that Mila was alone in the car with Jennifer as they drove back to her place. Mila wanted to protest at the silliness of all four of them coming to get her from the hospital when, really, it was no big deal. When she mumbled something about it, however, Jennifer cut all noise from the radio and scoffed.

"You can't understand how we feel about you getting out of there, Mila. I know this feels like a Herculean task for you, getting better and learning to walk again. But the four of us have hardly slept a wink. We'll sleep a little better knowing you're right there on Witchwood Lane, the way you always were before."

Jennifer parked in the familiar driveway of the house Peter had purchased for Mila, Isabelle, and Zane. Mila closed and opened her hands nervously as Jennifer leaped out and immediately broke into conversation with what sounded like Amelia and Camilla, who discussed the "bad traffic" on their way into Edgartown. Mila hadn't noticed the stops and starts. She supposed now it was a testament to Jennifer's driving and that she'd been conscious of the uncomfortable Mila in the backseat.

Tenderly, Jennifer and Camilla assisted Mila back into the wheelchair. Once seated, Mila took in full view of her house on Witchwood. If she closed her eyes just so, she could almost hear the call of her husband's voice coming from the backyard. *"What? What did you say, Peter? I can't hear you. I'll come around."*

Mila had been in frequent correspondence with her children since their return to school. Now that she had returned to Witchwood, however, Mila's heart felt bruised with the realization that she'd turned them away. How she longed to splay herself on the couch with her two silly wannabe adults, flip through television stations, and eat junk.

Camilla tapped the code into the garage door. The garage door erupted from the ground to reveal the dark shadows within.

Slowly, Jennifer wheeled Mila through that garage, which seemed haunted with old basketballs and other people's memories.

"All right. Are you ready?" Jennifer breathed in expectation as Olivia positioned a wheelchair ramp between the garage floor and the doorway that led into the main house, which was technically two steps up.

Camilla opened the door that led between the kitchen and living areas as Jennifer eased the wheelchair up the ramp. How ridiculous that it took such effort to get from the garage to the living room. Mila had never thought twice about those steps before. Now, they were like mountains.

Once inside, however, Mila breathed a sigh as she took in the full splendor of what her girls had done for her.

In the corner, a Christmas tree had been set up and decorated with all of Mila's favorite Christmas decorations, including the ones that reminded her most of Peter, Zane, and Isabelle. Her Christmas family portrait had been hung in the living room, a beautiful reminder of better times, and Christmas cookies had just come out of the oven and sat cooling on the countertop in all shapes of Christmas trees and reindeers and snowmen. Stockings hung from the fireplace, proof that this was a home that had once focused solely on the love within it.

Mila was terribly quiet as she took in every detail. Her eyes filled with tears, which she again refused to let fall.

"What do you think?" Jennifer stepped forward to peer into Mila's eyes. Fear permeated in her own.

"It's perfect," Mila breathed. "Really."

"I hope it's not too much," Jennifer murmured.

"It is. It always is too much," Mila replied with a laugh.

"Come on. Let's get her situated on the couch. We thought we'd frost the Christmas cookies when they cool down, sip some wine, and watch a Christmas movie together over the next few hours," Camilla suggested brightly.

"And then I guess you're off for the rehearsal dinner?" Mila asked.

"That's right. It's the beginning of the end," Camilla affirmed. "And in a funny way, I already feel sad that it's almost over."

"After all that complaining?" Amelia gave Camilla a crooked smile.

"I'm sorry, Amelia. Is this the first time you've met Camilla?" Jennifer teased. "I should have introduced you before..."

Amelia swatted her as she headed belly-first toward the kitchen, where she selected a still-cooling Christmas cookie and tore into it. "You've outdone yourself again, Olivia."

Olivia's eyes brightened. "I was dreaming about next Christmas at the Hesson House. Can you imagine the interior decorated with Christmas trees and holly and bright red ribbon? All those people coming and going as the snow falls around the mansion..."

"It sounds like a fantasy world," Mila tried. "And one I've very much excited to walk into with my own two legs."

Chapter Eleven

Isabelle's bedroom was an explosion of teenage angst and glitter. Band posters hung crooked on two opposite walls, seemingly in competition to be the messier one, and her four-poster bed was reminiscent of her princess-past, when she had donned little dresses and flounced around the house, hunting for compliments. "Like mother, like daughter," Amelia had teased at the time, only for Mila to nod, "Yes. She's got her mother's vanity, all right." Now, as Jennifer adjusted to the soft light of the morning, Isabelle's horrendous teenage-angst-decor reminded Jennifer of the flurry of events that led her to now.

It was Andrea's wedding day— a day meant for laughter and beautiful promises and bubbling champagne. How difficult to find the strength to celebrate as you carried the weight of the fate that had come before.

But thus far, the Sisters of Edgartown had handled Mila's care just fine. It had been a beautiful afternoon of Christmas cookies and wine and gut-busting giggles. Camilla had departed to prepare for the rehearsal dinner around five, which had left Jennifer, Amelia, and Olivia to squabble over how to do the next elements of the evening. Namely, they'd needed to help Mila figure out a bathing situation that suited her best without making her feel more shame than was necessary. Afterward, they'd wheeled her into the bedroom she had once shared with Peter and helped her nestle between the freshly-changed sheets. There, with her head deep on the cloud-like pillow, Jennifer had seen her more like a child than a woman of forty-one. She had seemed meek and helpless, and she knew Mila resented this. "Get out of here before you read me a bedtime story, too," Mila had kidded as the other three headed out, closing the door behind them.

Now, Jennifer tip-toed down the hallway of Mila's shadowed home on Witchwood. Once in the kitchen, she brewed a pot of coffee and texted with Nick for a moment, who reported that Stacy's morning sickness had finally subsided.

NICK: She says she's ready to eat her weight in wedding cake today, so everyone watch out.

Jennifer chuckled inwardly before she texted the others in the group chat, the one they'd recently created that didn't include Mila. It had felt dishonest to do this, going behind her back, but it had been the only way to arrange who-helped-with-what and when. Amelia's spreadsheet only went so far— and Jennifer didn't want a single dip in the quality of their care. Obviously, Mila's mother and sisters would help out here and there, as well, which Mila had called, "An anxious alternative but maybe a necessary reminder that even as I'm getting well after an accident, it still might never be enough for my mother." This had led Jennifer to insist that she, Olivia, Amelia, and Camilla do the brunt of the work.

"Good morning, Mila." Jennifer greeted Mila from the doorway of Mila's master bedroom as the door creaked open, casting light across the bedspread.

Mila groaned from between the sheets. "I gotta say. I'm not pleased to tell you this, but I need to go to the bathroom. Like, right now."

Jennifer's heart quickened. This was exactly the moment she had considered before trying to offer care without causing more shame than necessary. Hurriedly, she positioned the wheelchair alongside Mila's thin frame and assisted her into the chair, using much more of her strength than Jennifer had even thought she had. She then wheeled Mila to the master bathroom, where they had set up several railings to allow Mila to lift herself from the wheelchair to the toilet and back again.

Even still, the process was new. Mila muttered, "Can you just wait outside? Just in case I tumble to my death..."

"Of course," Jennifer breathed as she headed out. "Don't worry."

She wanted to tell Mila that she would do anything for her—that she would love her every day of her life, no matter what, as they aged and lost all control of their bodies, as time took over them and left them no relief.

Jennifer and Mila sat at the kitchen table over croissants with butter, fresh fruit, various cheeses, a pot of coffee, and just the tiniest sprinkling of champagne with orange juice.

"It's a celebration of many different things," Jennifer

explained. "It's your first morning back at your house, and it's the day Andrea marries the love of her life."

"A worthy day for a mimosa. Not that you needed to twist my arm." Mila delivered her first sterling smile of the morning, one that almost reached her eyes.

Prior to the accident, Mila had selected a navy blue, low-cut gown for Andrea's wedding. Jennifer told her that she saw no reason Mila couldn't still wear the dress.

"It was simple on the bottom, anyway," Jennifer stated as she lifted it from the closet after breakfast.

"You're right. It was always meant to be breast-first," Mila teased.

"And if there's anything you can brag about..." Jennifer returned with a wink.

"It's what I always told the girls in cheerleading, remember? Flaunt what you got," Mila said.

Jennifer helped Mila don the navy gown before she slipped into her own dark green dress, which had a high lace neckline and a cinched waist.

"I forgot you bought that," Mila told Jennifer as she reappeared. "Makes your eyes really pop."

"You were the one who forced me to buy it," Jennifer remembered. "You were like— Jen, if you don't buy that for Andrea's wedding, you'll regret it every day of your life."

Mila laughed. "I have a way of making shopping way more dramatic than it really is."

An hour before departure time, Amelia arrived in her wedding best, a burgundy maternity gown that swirled around her knees.

She pointed to her flats and said, “I can’t believe I’m wearing these to such a fancy occasion.”

“No pregnant woman should ever wear heels,” Mila confirmed with authority. “Pregnancy is cruel enough.”

“Olivia said she’s meeting us there,” Amelia said as she wiped down the counter of Mila’s kitchen to distract herself. “Chelsea is the maid of honor, and Olivia had to help her with a few things before the ceremony starts.”

“It’ll be good to see Chelsea again,” Mila breathed. “Sometimes I get all caught up in a fantasy of being her age, making it work with some handsome guy in Brooklyn.”

“I think there are a lot more rats in reality than in your fantasy,” Jennifer blurted.

“And cockroaches,” Amelia added as she scrunched her nose.

Mila tossed her head back. “Sometimes, I regret that I didn’t do something like that, rats and all.”

“Well, if Isabelle really makes it in the modeling industry, I guess she’ll have a loft for us to crash at in the city,” Jennifer countered.

“And glamorous parties to invite us to.” Mila’s smile was infectious. “It’s funny how angry I was at the concept of her dropping out to pursue modeling. The reality is, I know life doesn’t have a necessary timeline. I married a man twenty years my senior for crying out loud. College will always be there for Isabelle if she wants to go back to it.” Mila pressed her lips together tightly as her face shifted in color.

Jennifer could feel the memory of Mila and Isabelle’s argument stirring around in Mila’s mind. She knew those thoughts of the accident would stay permanently in Mila's head and threaten to come back anytime.

Jennifer had grown accustomed, now, to lifting Mila in and out of her wheelchair. She slipped Mila into the backseat of Amelia's car and folded together the wheelchair like an accordion before she joined Amelia in the front. Amelia said what you're always meant to say before such occasions: "I remember when she just learned to talk. Now she's getting married. What next?"

"What's next is your baby getting married," Jennifer countered. "It happens just like that." She snapped her fingers.

Andrea's wedding was held at the Edgartown Presbyterian Church, where already, nearly fifty vehicles had parked in the parking lot in preparation for the big day. Claire of the Oak Bluffs flower shop hovered outside of her business van, where she shifted through her wedding flower delivery bouquets which consisted of baby's breath, beautiful bouquets of white lilies for the bridesmaids and a much larger one for the bride herself. Claire waved a distracted hand at Amelia and Jennifer just before they helped Mila slip back into her wheelchair. At that sight, Claire's lips formed a round O.

As they wheeled past, Claire beamed with early afternoon greetings.

"So good to see you, Mila. You look beautiful."

Mila glowered for a split second before righting her face. "And you, Claire."

But when they were out of earshot, Mila muttered, "It's so weird to be the spectacle of the island this week."

"It'll pass. Everyone will get used to it," Amelia murmured.

Jennifer understood the weight of other people's perceived

kindnesses. Sometimes, they went so above and beyond that it felt suffocating.

Once at the church, Jennifer eased Mila's wheelchair up the ramp as Amelia waddled up behind them. Once in the foyer, one of Jonathon's brothers handed them a pamphlet before they were shown to their seats. Mila's wheelchair hovered off to the right of the row as Amelia and Jennifer seated themselves beside her. Very soon after, Derek, Nick, and Stacy arrived to slide in behind them, whispering excitedly.

When Stacy complimented Mila's dress, Derek took the opportunity to lean up to whisper in Jennifer's ear.

"How did it go last night?"

Jennifer nodded just the slightest bit to confirm that they'd gotten through just fine.

"Good. I missed you," he whispered.

"I have to admit, I'm glad it's not our wedding day," Nick admitted then.

Stacy gave him a playful smack across the hand. "What is that supposed to mean?"

"A man's wedding day is one of the most nerve-racking days of his life," Derek affirmed.

"Yeah? You're talking to the bride who was secretly three months pregnant and taking breaks to get sick in the bathroom between photo sessions on her wedding day," Stacy countered.

"Touché," Derek returned with a knowing smile.

Mila and Jennifer shared a wide grin over Stacy's sassiness. They didn't have to say what they both thought: that the girl seemed to sizzle with the same spark they'd had at that age.

Olivia and Anthony joined their group a few minutes later.

Anthony's suit highlighted his broad shoulders and surging muscles, which he'd built from his many months of fixing up the old Hesson House prior to its untimely demise in the hurricane. He greeted the other Sisters warmly and slid his fingers through Olivia's. She beamed with pride.

"Chelsea looks like a dream," she told them. "Andrea's on the verge of freaking out, but I think she'll pull it together enough to walk down the aisle."

"Oh, brother," Amelia giggled.

Instead of a five-piece string instrumental group, Andrea had opted for a pianist and a singer, who sang a beautiful love song in Italian as the groomsmen walked the bridesmaids down the aisle.

"Did we make the wrong choice with what we did?" Stacy whispered to Nick.

"Don't tell me we have to do the whole thing over again just because you like this singer better than the quintet," Nick returned.

"Yours was beautiful," Jennifer affirmed. "This is just different."

"Oh no. I think your mother agrees with me," Stacy muttered to Nick playfully.

"Shhh." A woman two rows behind them demanded they be quiet. Collectively, the four sisters, including Mila, blushed like children.

"We always get in trouble like this," Olivia explained to Anthony. "At this point, I'd consider it a failed wedding if someone didn't scold us."

After Chelsea walked down the aisle, turned on her heel, and beamed out across the crowd, the wedding song shifted. The organist played the classic wedding march to bring Andrea, flanked by both Camilla and Jonathon, out into the aisle.

The other Sisters had seen Andrea in her wedding dress prior to this fateful day, but the effect of it here, in the Presbyterian church, as the December light glittered through the stained-glass windows, was truly spectacular. Jennifer held her breath as the three members of Camilla's never-perfect but always-beautiful nuclear family reached the front of the gorgeous church.

Andrea turned toward her beloved, Isaac, who stretched out his palms so that she could slip her small hands over his. Their eyes met as the music stopped and the silence stretched across the crowd. Very soon, they would be united as husband and wife. Soon, their promise would be legal and binding— but a representation of the kind of love that was freeing in every way.

Chapter Twelve

The girls had done their very best to include Mila in every portion of the wedding ceremony and subsequent reception, which was held at a small event space attached to the Katama Lodge and Wellness Spa, located on the western edge of Katama Bay, just south of Edgartown. That said, the girls' best simply wasn't enough to blot out the misery that seemed to grow deeper within Mila as time passed. Jennifer and Mila's clunky morning routine had started things off slightly sour, at least for Mila, and things had just trucked along from there.

Now, mid-way through the reception itself, Mila tried her best to sit like a poised lady in a wheelchair. She had searched for images of "beautiful women in wheelchairs" the previous evening while she'd lay in bed alone and discovered that there was a sharpness to these women, a sign of courage that lurked behind their eyes. Maybe the courage came later, or maybe it was better to fake it till it came.

It was a couple's dance. From her stance at the side of the beautiful dance floor, Mila caught sight of Jennifer and Derek, lost in their swirling, frenetic conversation, captivated with one another's relative new perspective in their lives. Just a few couples away, Camilla and Jonathon danced with goofy grins, both grateful they'd thrown together a wedding after the year they'd had. Olivia and Anthony danced, as well, with Olivia's rather short skirt highlighting the athleticism of her runner's legs. Mila's stomach burned with jealousy. She took another sip of wine and tried to collect these dark thoughts into the back corner of her mind.

It had been beautiful to watch Andrea walk down the aisle—beautiful to see her pledge her life to a man she loved and beautiful to witness Camilla as she wept with joy as the church bells chimed above them.

But in truth, as she sat in the silence of herself at the side of the reception now, Mila felt like a fool. In many ways, she wished she remained at the hospital, where her routine had been steadfast. It had been expected that she couldn't do much of anything—where nurses' assistance hadn't filled her with so much shame. How embarrassing that at one time, she'd been the fastest runner on the girls' cheerleading team, and now she couldn't even go to the bathroom alone.

Mila grabbed her phone and typed the twelfth message to Liam that day, none of which she'd actually sent but saved as drafts.

MILA: I wish you would just be man enough to tell me what's going on in your head.

This time, however, she took a long sip of wine and tapped her finger against the SEND button. If Liam wanted to act like an absolute trash bag of a human, she was willing to remind him of this fact.

Unfortunately, it seemed that Liam's phone was off or he'd blocked her. Her message received only one checkmark. She took another long swig of wine and cursed herself inwardly.

The wedding DJ announced that it was time for the bouquet toss. Camilla stepped out of the crowd of giggling women to join Mila.

"How are you holding up, honey?" Camilla asked warmly.

The last person Mila wanted to complain to was the mother of the bride, who would remember Mila's disappointment regarding her daughter's wedding forever if she brought it up now.

"It's a beautiful wedding. So glad I got to come," Mila replied, looking out at all the women getting ready to catch the bride's bouquet.

"Well, I'm sure you know already, but that dress is a knock-out." Camilla waved a hand toward a passing waiter, who arrived to refill both of their glasses. "Jennifer said things went pretty smoothly this morning?" Her eyes scanned the crowd as she was on constant wedding duty.

"Sure," Mila offered. "As smooth as anything."

"That's great, Mil. Really." Camilla waved a hand toward a family member and added, "Gosh, that's Jonathon's, Aunt Cherry. I'd better run off and greet her before she tells everyone on Jonathon's side of the family I snubbed her."

Mila's laughter rang false. "I remember all the in-law politics," she commented, although, in actuality, Peter's parents had both been dead when she had gotten involved with him.

She just wanted to feel a part of the club of those who loved, of those who were loved.

But you couldn't just wish yourself into that club.

Mila wheeled herself over to the cake table. An hour before, the crowd had gathered to watch as Andrea and her beloved had playfully smashed little frosted bits of cake into one another's faces. For their wedding, Mila had instructed Peter not to do that, as it would mess up her refined makeup look. He'd done it anyway — something she'd always half-appreciated, half-resented. It had seemed the perfect symbol of their marriage. The photo of the moment itself, her face aglow with shock, had graced Peter's work desk for decades, although she had begged him to remove it.

Her feelings for Liam could never have compared to her love for her husband. She knew that now. The feeling of it soured in her gut.

"Would you like a slice of cake, ma'am?" a waiter at the cake table leaned down slightly to speak to her. It was understandable, given that the event space was quite loud and it was difficult to hear. Even still, Mila resented it.

"No. No, thank you." Mila sipped her wine, then wheeled herself out toward the far outskirts of the crowd, where she made her way into the hallway, out of sight.

Once there, as the party swirled on, a chorus of laughter and funny conversation, Mila closed her eyes against it all and allowed herself to sob, really sob, in a way she hadn't since she had arrived home. At every turn, that sob had grown more powerful in the pit of her gut, and now, here it was. It was taking hold of her, just as Hurricane Janine had erupted over the island two months before.

Without knowing why, Mila lifted her phone and dialed a newer number.

"Mila? Is that you?" Hannah's voice rang through the darkness and lifted Mila's spirits. She sounded so happy to hear her, so thrilled that she'd reached out. At least Mila could be that for someone, rather than a burden.

"It sure is," Mila returned, wiping away her tears.

"I thought the wedding was today?"

"It is. I'm calling from outside."

"Oh goodness. And you thought of me? How lovely."

Mila leaned her head so that her hair shifted down the back of the chair, the chair she'd be latched to for the foreseeable future. She tried to picture Hannah's world, although she had never been to Hannah's house and, in truth, she had no idea where it was.

"What are you up to?" she asked.

"Oh, goodness, I'm a bit embarrassed to say. It's only eight, and I'm all tucked away for the night. Got my pajamas on and everything."

"I'm sure your pajamas are just about the most stylish pajamas around," Mila countered.

"They aren't bad. A little vintage get-up from the forties."

"I should have known." Mila grinned into the phone. Before she knew what she'd done, she found herself asking, "Why don't you come to the reception? There are still hours to go, and I'd love to see you."

Hannah was quiet for a moment. Something spat and crackled in the background, maybe a radio or a television.

"There's still plenty of food as well," Mila continued. "I'm sure I could get them to make you a plate. They'll do anything for the woman in the wheelchair."

Hannah's laughter was nervous but endearing. "They'd do anything for Mila, wheelchair or not." She paused for a moment, then added, "I really don't have anything to wear."

"That's ridiculous. I bet you have fifteen outfits ready to go right this minute and besides? When was the last time you went to a party?"

"Goodness me. It's probably been five years."

"Then it's about time, don't you think?"

To Mila's amazement, Hannah arrived at Andrea's reception forty-five minutes later. Just as Mila had suspected, her chosen outfit was the very best of fifties' fashion, with glowing, milky pearls and little pink high-heels. She glanced around the party nervously as her fingers cradled two of the pearls on her necklace.

"You're so beautiful, Hannah," Mila complimented with a wide smile. "I'm so glad you're here."

Mila gestured for a waiter to bring them a fresh glass of wine. Hannah giggled as she took her first sip.

"So many pretty people here, Mila. I recognize some of them from the salon."

"We do our best to make Martha's Vineyard a pretty place," Mila quipped. "Who knows what would happen if we closed up shop? The unibrow situation on this island would reach an epidemic level."

Hannah giggled good-naturedly. "Not to mention the upper-lip fuzz..."

"Hannah!" Mila's heart lifted with surprise.

Hannah shrugged as her lips flirted into a smile. "I'll never tell who, of course. A lady never reveals other ladies' beauty secrets."

"We should make that the salon slogan," Mila took a sip of her wine.

Hannah selected a seat at a round table that only had a few people sitting at it, which allowed Mila to glide up alongside her. Hannah pointed out Mila's friends, who had grown lost to the haze of wine and dancing with loved ones.

"Your friends have such life to them. How lucky you are!"

Mila tilted her head. "You're my friend, too, Hannah. I hope you know that."

Hannah seemed oddly flustered at the thought. She took a large sip of wine and muttered something about wanting a slice of cake but that she'd "better not." As Mila tried to drum up another topic of conversation, an older gentleman from Jonathon's side of the family stepped up to their table and pointed toward Hannah's already empty glass.

"Can I get you something to drink?" he asked her, ignoring Mila altogether and focusing his attention on the other beautiful woman before him.

Hannah's cheeks flushed crimson. "Oh goodness. I suppose so? It was the white wine. Chardonnay, I believe, not that I'm any wine snob or anything."

The man disappeared and returned with a glass for her and a fresh beer for himself. "Do you mind if I sit with you, two beautiful ladies?"

Hannah's eyes found Mila's. The strength of her gaze could have burned a hole in the ozone layer.

"Of course. Sit with us," Mila piped up as she recognized Hannah was too nervous to answer him.

The man sat and introduced himself as Thomas Wright. Hannah continued to be unable to meet his gaze, although he desperately tried to get her attention. He asked her how she knew the bride and groom, which led her to admit she didn't know either of them.

"She's my date," Mila offered brightly.

"Ah. I hope I'm not barking up the wrong tree," Thomas said.

"You're not." Hannah looked as though she couldn't believe she'd just offered up that information about her personal life. Her eyes widened as she slowly turned her head to face him.

"Then I wonder if I might have the pleasure of asking you to dance?"

Hannah gulped and nodded her head slowly, tentatively, as she rose from her chair. Thomas stood up with more youth and vitality than his sixty-plus years should have allowed.

"Will you be okay, Mila?" Hannah's voice wavered.

"Of course," Mila returned with an earnest smile.

Thomas stepped out toward the floor as Hannah bent down to whisper in Mila's ear.

"I really can stay with you. I don't mind. I'm sure he's just trying to be nice to an old lady."

Mila shook her head. "Hannah, you're a knock-out. This is fun. Let yourself have fun for a change. You deserve it."

Hannah rose back up, gave Mila a determined nod, and turned

to meet Thomas, who placed his hand at the base of her back and then whirled her into the crowd.

Mila's heart pounded so loudly, as though she was deep underwater and could hear only that. She took an additional sip of wine and felt herself fall deeper into the depths of some kind of despair. Maybe it was the kind of despair that would become familiar to her, as natural and easy as an old friend.

Chapter Thirteen

December 15th

It had been nearly three weeks since the accident and nearly two since Mila had returned home to heal. It also happened to be Jennifer's forty-second birthday, yet another date to mark the passage of time and the years she'd had to live apart from Michelle. How reckless and idiotic they'd been all those years ago to let her go like that. Sometimes, it still burned Jennifer with a rage she couldn't shift away from, not very easily anyway. Michelle should have been with all of them, this and every other day. She should have been allowed to turn forty-two years old.

Jennifer awoke on the morning of her forty-second birthday to an elaborate breakfast crafted from Derek's own two hands: fluffy pancakes and bright red strawberries and greasy sausages and glittering mimosas. It was a Wednesday, and Jennifer had squelched all meetings and work events from her calendar in pursuit of the perfect, relaxing day.

"Mmm." She chewed the dripping-with-syrup pancake with closed eyes. When she opened them, she refocused to discover a beautiful image. The dark clouds' ever-constant sleet of the previous week had transformed to large fluffy snowflakes.

Always, when it snowed on her birthday, she felt it was Michelle saying hello to her in the only way she could.

"It's beautiful," Jennifer whispered as she placed a slice of strawberry on her tongue. Hope swelled in her stomach.

That morning, Mila had an appointment at the hospital to go over her recent progress and meet with the hospital psychologist. After her breakfast (and an additional hour in bed with Derek), Jennifer showered and headed off to take over Amelia's position at Mila's house.

In the past week, Mila had insisted on hiring a nurse for occasional assistance, which had eased the schedule on the rest of the Sisters. Since then, there had been a lighter quality to Mila's conversation. Perhaps their constant attentiveness had made Mila feel guilty and useless. It was difficult for Jennifer to put herself in Mila's shoes.

"Happy birthday, beautiful!" Amelia and Mila greeted Jennifer warmly upon their arrival. Amelia handed her a little cupcake, on which they'd drawn a J in pink frosting over the top base of buttercream frosting.

"This is sinful," Jennifer breathed.

"We have more for tonight," Amelia told her. "We baked them last night."

"And there's a whole lot more where they came from," Mila

added with a sneaky smile. "You know, it's tradition to eat our weight in garbage on your and Michelle's birthday."

It was always a remarkable thing to hear Michelle's name again. It was as though, in that split-second, she was allowed to live on again.

With Mila in the front seat of Jennifer's car and her wheelchair safely in the back trunk, the girls fell into easy conversation. Although Mila's journey remained long and difficult and terrifying, each day brought them closer, and there was joy in the in-between if they helped Mila look for it.

"I'm actually sleeping through the night. And I can feel the muscles in my forearms getting stronger and more powerful," Mila explained brightly as she lifted an arm to fake-flex.

Jennifer waited outside of Mila's psychologist appointment, where she received a call first from her mother, then from her father, then from her son, as though they had all wanted to get the obligatory birthday phone call out of the way at once.

Nick sang her a little "Happy Birthday" song, just as he always had since he'd been a little boy.

"Remember when you kept forgetting the words and would instead insert words from songs you knew better, like 'Twinkle Twinkle Little Star'?" Jennifer teased as he finished up.

"You always remind me of that, every year, without fail," Nick returned, feigning exasperation. "Are we still on for lunch tomorrow? I know you have your traditions to take care of."

"We're still on. I wouldn't miss a free lunch from my son or his company."

Mila chatted to her daughter on the drive back to Mila's place. Jennifer listened to the funny shriek of Isabelle as she explained the intricacies of the last week of her first semester of college. Mila beamed as she fell silent and allowed Isabelle's story to roll over her. When she finally managed to get off the phone, she clucked her tongue and said, "That girl is on her way somewhere. Where, exactly, I have no idea."

"Modeling career?"

"She really got back into her poetry class the past few weeks. Her professor wants her to take a series of upper-level classes next semester instead of the curriculum she'd set out for."

"You must be happy?"

Mila's smile curved toward her ears. "She could tell me she's going to move to the moon and I'd be supportive. That fight... It changed everything for us."

Jennifer wanted to say something about how big events in people's families shifted things either one way or the other. They allowed either increased compassion or else brought about fear and volatility and anger. Michelle's death had been like a bomb going off in the Conrad family, an explosion from which they'd never fully recovered. They hadn't found compassion for many years, and sometimes, they had to really work for it.

Olivia, Camilla, and Amelia arrived at Mila's place for the birthday festivities just past five that evening. December light was ghoulish and strange, and, as the snow hadn't held up, rain pattered across the windowpanes. They wrapped themselves in Mila's wide selection of cozy blankets and perched on the couch and the cushy chairs, forming a circle that included Mila's wheelchair. Olivia played old nineties tunes they'd once loved and shoved the first "appetizer" into the oven as she opened a bottle of wine.

"What's on the menu first?" Jennifer called.

"Mozzarella sticks and jalapeno poppers!" Olivia returned from the kitchen.

"My poor baby," Amelia jested with a laugh. "All I've had is green smoothies and nut butter for the past seven months."

"If your baby's going to hang with us, she or he better get used to the occasional mozzarella stick," Mila countered. "Besides. Life is about balance. You know that."

As Olivia poured the wine glasses, they caught one another up on their weekly activities. Mila was the common denominator amongst all of them, as they all saw her one-on-one throughout their schedules. She was, therefore, the ultimate therapist when it came to things like work and marriage conflicts, as she'd heard all their stories again and again.

"You should really start a talk show." Olivia entered with the first round of wine glasses. "You've got that sharp wit and enough good advice to get people back on their feet again."

"Plus, you could give fashion and makeup advice," Camilla agreed, taking her glass from Olivia.

Mila laughed. "I don't know about that. But goodness, I would love to do something like 'What Not to Wear.' Raid people's closets and get them to throw out all their terrible clothes. I think it's so freeing to reinvent yourself like that and actually think about how you want to present yourself to the world." Her right finger traced a line down her wheelchair's wheel. "I've been thinking about getting some more wheelchair-friendly outfits. I even started a little online blog about what to wear when you're wheelchair-bound. I found so many women online curious about this very topic."

"That's beautiful, Mila," Jennifer breathed.

"I had to figure out something to do with all this free time," Mila joked. "Besides, if I never learn to walk again..."

"Don't talk like that," Olivia scolded.

"It's a very real possibility, and I have to find peace with it sooner or later," Mila countered. "If I never learn to walk again, I want to be the best-dressed wheelchair-owner on the island of Martha's Vineyard, at least. Maybe on the eastern seaboard."

"Hear, hear," Jennifer returned as she lifted her glass of wine to salute her.

The others joined and held their glasses aloft for a moment before Mila blushed and said, "But enough about me. This day is all about our girls. Jennifer and Michelle. Happy forty-second. How time flies when you're having fun with your soulmates."

The girls agreed, dipped their heads back, and drank. This term, soulmate, sizzled in the back of Jennifer's mind. In the previous few weeks, she hadn't seen nor heard from Liam, the police officer. Mila hadn't mentioned him either, and Jennifer had sensed to keep her distance from the topic.

The other girls had noticed, too. And now, Amelia dragged up the courage to ask.

"Mila? Do you mind if we ask you something?"

Mila pressed her lips together as fear permeated her face. "Okay. You can."

Amelia's eyes shifted. "What happened with Liam? He came up the night of the accident and waited around until we knew you were okay. I saw him a few times after that, but..."

Mila's cheeks became blotchy and red. She sipped her wine again as her eyes glossed over.

"I don't really know, to be honest with you," she whispered. "He finally called the other day. I hadn't heard from him in ages."

"God, that snake," Camilla muttered.

Mila shrugged. "He explained that he has a bit of PTSD from some of his earlier days as a cop in Boston. When I was injured so badly, it triggered some stuff for him."

"Still... that has nothing to do with your relationship," Camilla protested.

Mila closed her eyes tightly. A storm rolled over her and made her shoulders shake. "I thought maybe I could love him. I'm just frankly glad he showed me this side of himself. This side that just couldn't take the hard stuff between us."

"So... it's over?" Jennifer asked, aghast.

Mila nodded as the first tear fell. "You four have been such a dream throughout all of this. Every one of you is always there for me at my beck and call, trying your darnedest to make me feel normal in the midst of so much turmoil and strangeness. But Liam made me feel like I was a burden that he didn't know how to deal with. I think deep down, he just didn't know how to deal with the situation and it freaked him out. How are you supposed to fall in love with something like that or vice versa? I don't want to involve myself with anyone like that."

"I'm so sorry, sweetie. That's not right and it's probably a good thing it's happening early on in the relationship rather than later. It just makes it easier to let go," Camilla affirmed.

"Maybe. Maybe not." Mila sniffled. "All I can say is, I don't feel particularly into the dating scene as a woman laid up in a wheelchair. If I don't get back on my feet, that will be another question. Do I date again in a wheelchair? Do I focus on other things? I don't know."

The Sisters were quiet for a moment. Jennifer hadn't known all this had lurked in Mila's mind over the past few weeks. Jennifer recognized, now, just how much Mila had had to protect the four of them, even as they had struggled to try to protect her with their strict schedules and their home-cooked meals.

"You will find a way through this," Jennifer assured her then. "You're stronger than all of us put together. If you want to date, you'll date. If you don't want to date, you'll rule the world some other way. Whatever will be, will be."

Mila's eyes shone as her lower lip quivered.

"I had a dream about Michelle the other night," she told them.

Jennifer's ears twitched. She'd occasionally had dreams about her twin during times of strife, as though the universe itself wanted to communicate something enormous.

"She and I were on that old dock they've since removed. The one near the sailboat docks," Mila continued. "We were both young but not overly so, maybe twenty-five, and we ran and jumped into the water over and over again until we became tired. We then floated on our backs and held hands and gazed at the blue sky up above. In this world, there was never winter, only summer... only life. And at the end of the dream, she told me to let go of her hand. I told her no way. I wouldn't do it. And she tried to tug it away from me as hard as she could until suddenly, I woke up. And..."

Mila trailed off again as her tears caught the soft light.

"And I swear, as I lay in my bed alone, I felt her hand in mind.

I swear to you four. She was here with me. And I've felt her with us ever since."

The girls leaped from their chairs and collected themselves around Mila's wheelchair. The next few minutes became tear-filled smiles and the kind of hugs that negated all the fear in the universe. It was still the very beginning of what would be a very beautiful night, during which they would collect the pieces of their broken parts and slowly fit them back together again, just as they always had before.

Chapter Fourteen

Just as tradition called for, the five Sisters of Edgartown crashed together in a sleepover reminiscent of their middle school days. Each slept heavily, their stomachs filled to the brim with mozzarella sticks and pizza slices and gummy bears and wine.

Jennifer awoke just past seven to find Amelia already up and at-em in the kitchen. She sliced strawberries and listened to a podcast on her headphones, one about preparation for childbirth and the first months of her baby's life. When she spotted Jennifer in the doorway, she leaped with surprise.

"You thought you were the only early riser around here?" Jennifer teased.

Amelia placed her headphones across the counter. "I couldn't sleep past six. This baby of mine would not stop dancing in my stomach. It also doesn't help that she or he is pressing right on my bladder."

"Oh, God. I don't miss those days of constantly peeing and not finding a comfortable position to sleep at night." Jennifer stepped toward the coffee maker to brew up a pot. As the black liquid flicked into the glass container, she lifted her arms to stretch.

"I want to kill Liam for what he did to Mila," Amelia confessed as she blew out the remaining breath in her mouth.

Jennifer grimaced. "In all my years, I never imagined someone treating Mila like that."

"Not our Mila," Amelia added.

Jennifer's nostrils flared. She reached for her phone, which had remained on its charger since the previous afternoon. When she turned it on, she found several texts, all from Derek and all after one a.m. Her heart pumped with fear.

"What's wrong, Jen?" Amelia demanded. "I don't like the expression you're wearing."

DEREK: Hey! Nick just got here.

DEREK: He looked upset. I don't know what is going on.

DEREK: I told him he could sleep in the guest room for the night.

DEREK: Anyway - I love you so much. I can't wait to celebrate your birthday a little bit more, just the two of us.

Jennifer furrowed her brow. "Nick came back to Derek and I's place last night..."

"Really? That's bizarre. Is Stacy out of town?"

"Not that I know of." Jennifer glanced back toward Mila's living room, where Camilla was all stretched out on the couch and Olivia slept on a blow-up mattress, just like old times. Mila remained in her bed while Amelia had slept in Zane's room and Jennifer in Isabelle's.

"If you need to head home and figure this out, I'll explain it to the others," Amelia offered.

"Yes. I think that is probably a good idea. I'm just... He's not normally like this."

Jennifer did her best to tend to her face and makeup, her motions blurry with panic. When she jumped back in her vehicle, the radio spat out news of a robbery over in Oak Bluffs. Two criminals had broken into an older couple's home with the mind to steal their silverware and jewelry. They'd been captured in the midst of the act, as their neighbor had been out with his dog. Jennifer shivered at the story. Cruelty hit them everywhere — even on Martha's Vineyard, a supposedly fairytale of a place.

Jennifer tried to explain the facts to herself en route to the condo if only to calm her racing mind. Nick was safe. Probably, he was still asleep, as he'd never gotten over that pubescent desire to sleep the hours away. Stacy had laughed about this recently, saying he would sleep till noon every day if he could.

Nick wasn't just safe, in fact. He'd headed straight for her place, rather than Joel's, when times had gotten tough.

Jennifer burst through the front door to find Derek at the breakfast table with a bowl of cereal and a spread-out newspaper before him. He wore only a t-shirt and a pair of boxers, and he'd obviously ran his fingers through his hair many times as he'd struggled through the crossword. Jen's heart brewed with love at the sight of him. She dropped down and kissed him tenderly on the cheek, then glanced toward the shadows of the hall.

"Any sign of him?"

"Not yet." Derek folded up his newspaper to give Jennifer his full attention. "I might have heard him crying earlier. Don't tell him I said that."

"Gosh." Jennifer pressed her teeth into her lower lip. It was only eight. She had to be patient. If he'd arrived so late to the house, he needed his sleep. Sorrow made a person sleepier anyway.

Jennifer poured herself a bowl of cereal and perched next to Derek to help him with the crossword. It was a way to pass the time, although it barely helped at all. Minutes dragged.

Around nine-thirty, after listening to a podcast and very nearly closing out the (admittedly difficult) crossword, a rustling came from the guest room. Jennifer froze as Nick bucked out to head for the bathroom. When he reappeared, his eyes locked onto hers. She knew this look — it was devastation.

Jennifer leaped up from her chair and walked to the bedroom, where he'd just disappeared. He sat at the edge of the bed in the darkness with his hands folded between his knees.

"Nick..." Jennifer stepped inside and hovered. "Do you mind if we talk?"

Nick shook his head. Jennifer closed the door softly behind her, conscious that Nick probably didn't want his mother's boyfriend to hear his secrets.

A beat passed, then another. Jennifer's throat tightened.

"Whatever it is, we can get through it together," Jennifer told him. "You aren't alone."

Again, silence. Nick exhaled all the air from his lungs. He still didn't have the strength to look her way.

"She lost the baby," Nick murmured finally.

Jennifer draped her hand over her heart. Her knees threatened to kick out beneath her. "When did it happen?"

"Yesterday morning," Nick whispered. "I rushed her to the hospital. She was three and a half months pregnant, Mom. We thought we were in the clear."

Jennifer dropped onto the bed alongside her son. Although they were incredibly common, Jennifer had never had a miscarriage and struggled not to find it one of the hardest-possible things imaginable. All this hope around a beautiful idea of a future, suddenly shattered, usually for unexplainable reasons.

"They released her from the hospital in the afternoon," Nick explained. "She wouldn't talk to me for an hour. After that, she got all ready to go and said she wanted to go to her parents' place. I told her we needed to sit together and process this together. But she was so devastated, rightfully so, but so am I. The hurt and sorrow that filled her eyes, I've never seen that type of pain before."

Nick wiped his fingers over his face. The images seemed too cruel.

"I told her she could take time at her parents if that's what she needs— that we can come back to one another this weekend and talk about everything. But she says she isn't sure about anything right now. Being with me reminds her of this life she dreamed of. And she just wants to be alone. Admittedly, it's been a whole lot of her and me the past few years. We neglected our other friendships under the belief that we only needed each other. Now, I feel so alone, to be honest with you. And I'm reminding her of one of the worst days of her life, of our life."

Jennifer rubbed Nick's upper back as he shook with his sobs.

Wasn't this meant to be a time for everyone to hold one another up? He moved his head toward her shoulder and huddled against her, which was an unusual sight, considering he was much bigger than his mother. It didn't matter.

"Nick. You know these things happen," Jennifer breathed. "Miscarriages are common, even at this stage of the game. It's absolutely awful, but it doesn't change anything between you and Stacy. She'll realize she needs your support in this. She's just taking some time."

"It just kills me that she won't let me care for her," Nick replied. "We only got married a few weeks ago. I pledged to love and support her all the days of my life. And now, here I am in your guest bedroom, waiting for her to call."

"She will call," Jennifer affirmed. "And when the time comes, you will get pregnant again. You both are still so young, Nick. I know it probably doesn't feel that way right now. But when you get as old as me, you realize the length of time. There's so much of it, with so much set aside for mistakes and screw-ups and natural disasters, like this one. If you want to, you and Stacy still have time to have upwards of ten kids."

Nick let out an ironic laugh. "Don't get ahead of yourself, Mom. We agreed on three tops."

"See? You can probably get three in before you turn twenty-seven. I never dared for more than one. Me and your dad always said you were our perfect miracle baby. Besides that, you had this really awful streak at the age of three when we couldn't get you to stop screaming for hours at a time. That put us off kids as well."

Nick puffed out his cheeks. Jennifer wasn't sure if these stories were helping or hurting. Even still, it was better than the silences, which seemed to darken the air.

"Let me make you some breakfast, Nicky," Jennifer suggested while rubbing his arm in comfort.

"I don't know. I'm not sure I can eat," Nick told her.

"My son can always eat. It's a fact of life," Jennifer stated in a firmer tone. "Plus, you'll make yourself so upset if you don't fuel your body. Really, Nick. Just let me make you an omelet."

Nick feigned annoyance, even as he gave her his first real smile of the morning.

"Okay. Fine. If you insist."

Back in the kitchen, Jennifer cracked eggs into a glass bowl and muttered the news under her breath so that Derek understood. His eyes were heavy with sorrow.

"He must know that this is common?"

"I don't think it matters right now. He just wants to be there for Stacy, and all Stacy wants is space," Jennifer returned.

Jennifer positioned onions and peppers and zucchini across the wooden cutting board and took solace in the repetitive motions and the sharp slice of the knife. Mid way through the onion, she received a text from the group chat, which included a photo of the four of them over breakfast.

MILA: Miss you, girl. I hope everything's okay.

CAMILLA: And happy birthday! We love you.

OLIVIA: Forever.

AMELIA: And ever!

Jennifer showed Derek the photo of the four of them and their fluffy pancakes and their bright strawberries.

"Not one of you look like you ate your weight in gummy bears last night," Derek teased gently. "What's your secret?"

"We're witches, of course."

Nick, Jennifer, and Derek sat around the kitchen table in their pajamas and feasted on omelets heaped with sour cream and salsa. Nick stirred them up some mimosa's mid-way through their meal, even as Derek protested that he "had to do a little bit of work later."

"It's a Thursday for some of us around here," Derek pointed out.

"It's still kind of my birthday," Jennifer returned with a funny smirk.

"Oh, great. How long are you going to use that excuse?" Derek laughed outright as Nick placed his drink before him on the table.

"As long as I can get away with it," Jennifer said with a wink.

Bit-by-bit, as they fueled themselves over breakfast, Nick's skin brightened. His smile came in, stops and starts. To take his mind off of things, Derek told Nick a number of stories from his early days in New York City.

"Don't let him get any ideas," Jennifer scolded. "I won't make it if my only kid runs off the island."

"You know I couldn't make it out there," Nick told her.

"Make it? You could make it, kid," Derek affirmed. "The fact is, though, life's borderline paradise around here. Now that I live here more or less full-time, I don't want a life anywhere else. Emma's talked about moving out here, too."

"It's funny to think about everything I had growing up that other people just didn't have," Nick said thoughtfully. "It was kind of special, wasn't it? The beaches and the sailboats and the seafood. There's always magic on the island during those months."

"And a different kind of magic here around Christmas," Derek added. "I felt it first thing last year, around the time I met your mom."

Jennifer blushed. "Someone's a sap this morning."

Derek laughed as he lifted another forkful of the omelet to his lips. "So, sue me. I'm a sap. Never advertised myself as anything but a sap."

"Yeah! Me too!" Nick chimed in brightly. "It's good we can support each other."

"Just us saps against the cruel world," Derek agreed.

Chapter Fifteen

The Edgartown Christmas Festival was an annual two-week-long celebration, which stretched from before Christmas till just before New Year's Eve and incorporated a number of Edgartown and Oak Bluffs businesses, each at little booths and stands. For sale was hot mulled wine and cider, burritos and clam chowder and fresh fish and other traditional island fare, all for take-away, for dining along the streets with other islanders. It was a tradition for the Sisters of Edgartown to gather together to bundle up and feast on their favorite island fare as they wandered around the streets. Miraculously, despite Amelia's pregnancy and Mila's wheelchair, Jennifer had basically insisted they continue on with tradition. "We'll take as many breaks as we need, but we need this, ladies— to feed our souls."

The day before the girls planned to attend the festival, Mila was at home alone for the first time in what seemed like ages. She wheeled herself around sleepily, checked the fridge just like any other version of Mila, then decided instead on a small glass of wine. She perched her wheelchair in front of her television and flicked through the stations as she sipped. In a little more than an hour, Olivia planned to swing by to pick her up for a rehabilitation appointment up at the hospital.

Twenty minutes later, there was a knock at the front door. Mila wheeled herself over, opened the door, and found not Olivia, but Hannah from the salon instead. As usual, she was dressed in what seemed like winter couture, and her beautiful white hair caught the gleam of the snow perfectly. Hannah's smile was infectious.

"I hope you don't mind I stopped by like this," she asked as she stepped into the foyer. "I thought of you when I got off work and, well, I brought you some fresh pastries. Look at how adorable they are! They're a brand-new selection from the Sunrise Cove Bistro."

The fresh puff pastries were filled with chocolate and vanilla cream; the dough was flakey and sweet, the sort that immediately melted along your tongue. Hannah hurriedly positioned a few on one of Mila's deep blue plates and created a cafe-like ambiance for them in Mila's living room as Mila turned off the television. Hannah remained mostly quiet, muttering to herself quietly as she removed her coat and seated herself primly at the edge of the couch. Even after all their small encounters since Mila's stint in the hospital, Mila still found it incredibly difficult to picture the inner life of Hannah. She was a mystery.

"How is everything, Hannah?" Mila lifted a pastry and tore through the gloriously textured edge as her eyes closed, savoring the taste.

"Oh, just fine. Just fine. The salon is just about as busy as ever, although I'm sure you know that. There are so many women bustling in and out in preparation for the holidays. One woman I attended to yesterday had a tiny meltdown about her newly found wrinkles, as she said her mother-in-law is coming in from Boston and is terribly judgmental toward her." Hannah clucked her tongue sadly as she selected her own pastry. "Just a tragedy that these beautiful Christmas celebrations devolve to such fear of judgment and pettiness."

"Did you try to talk her down?"

"As best as I could," Hannah returned. "And we did a full-scale facial massage and treatment. She came out of there glowing like a teenager. I wanted to tell her how beautiful I find the aging process to be, especially at sixty-four and smack-dab in the middle of it. But I recognize that the first few years of it all bring a bout of growing pains."

"I can't imagine that you ever handled it with anything but grace," Mila countered.

Hannah's laughter was edged with sadness. It echoed back memories that Mila would probably never learn about the older woman.

"You know, Mila, I wanted to thank you again for inviting me to that splendid wedding." Hannah lowered her voice. "I keep dreaming about it. The magic of the music and that handsome man who whirled me around the dance floor. A woman like me never thought I'd had anything close to a fairytale again."

Mila wasn't sure what to say. After two or three dances, Hannah's dance partner had headed off for the night and left her captivated in a way she clearly couldn't shake. Was she delusional about what might happen?

"Don't worry, dear," Hannah affirmed, as though she read her mind. "I know very well that man is off the island and onto greener pastures. He's just left me with my daydreams, is all."

Mila's lips curved into a sorrowful smile. "I don't think there's anything greener than all this. Besides, why wouldn't he be captivated with you right back? You were and are a knock-out, Hannah. Truly."

Hannah's cheek twitched nervously. She wasn't so keen on compliments.

"Curious, Hannah. What are your plans for Christmas?"

Hannah waved a hand. "Oh, you know. I'll get together with a few loved ones. Swap some presents and some deliciously sinful food, just like everyone else."

Mila's heart lifted. "Who? People off the island coming in to see you?" She hadn't thought the older woman had any connections whatsoever besides her sister in California.

Hannah made a soft noise in her throat. "Sure thing. And how about you, honey? How are you spending your days? How's your pain?"

According to the doctor, Mila's body was a superstar in terms of proper healing. "They say I'm right on track," she explained. "I'm headed into the hospital to meet with a rehabilitation specialist. They want to help me to better walk on crutches here and there, so I can get myself around the house a bit better. The casts will come off in the new year sometime, which is around the time I'll start to relearn how to walk if you can believe it."

"Remarkable! Really, Mila, this is such splendid news."

Mila's laughter was almost sincere. So often, throughout conversations like this, her mind played wicked tricks on her and reminded her of all she had lost along the way. It was difficult, sometimes, to focus on the good.

"And how will you get to the hospital today?" Hannah asked as the silence stretched between them.

"Olivia plans to take me when she gets off of work. She works as an English teacher at the high school."

Hannah's eyes fell toward the half-eaten puff pastries between them.

"Well, honey, I would be happy to take you up there," Hannah replied then. "Since I'm already here and I don't have anything planned the rest of the day."

Mila had had a whole host of gossipy items to discuss with Olivia upon her arrival— stuff like what a recent actress had worn to a Christmas party (the most horrendous fake-fur get-up you've ever seen) and another celebrity's whispered divorce and also gossip she'd heard surrounding Jennifer's ex-husband, Joel, and the possibility that he and his girlfriend had recently broken up. Already, she had imagined herself saying to Olivia, *"I mean, come on. How does any woman follow up Jennifer Conrad?"*

But she could see the importance of this echoed back in Hannah's eyes. She needed to take Mila up to the hospital almost as much as Mila needed to go for her health.

"That would be great," Mila told her. "I'll text Olivia that she's off-duty."

Hannah was an incredibly conscious and safe driver. Mila watched as she eased just under the speed limit all the way from Edgartown to Oak Bluffs Hospital, where she paused the car around the drop-off lane and leaped up to grab Mila's wheelchair in the back. A hospital worker spotted them outside and rushed to assist Mila from the car to the wheelchair itself. Mila now recognized him as the twenty-year-old Greg, who teased her as she adjusted in the wheelchair.

"You just can't get enough of us these days, can you, Miss Mila?"

"You know I'm always here to see your handsome face, Gregory," she replied with a smile.

Hannah watched this exchange with wide eyes. After Greg disappeared down a hallway and left the two of them in the foyer, Hannah whispered, "Do you know everyone around here?"

"Not everyone," Mila laughed. "But I think they realize I'll get better faster if they laugh at my jokes."

They checked in at the front desk before heading to the nearby corner to wait for Mila's appointment. Directly beside them was an ancient coffee maker that required only a quarter for a small plastic cup. Hannah leafed through her vintage purse to find one before stuffing it in. When she grabbed her over-filled plastic cup of coffee, however, the hot plastic burnt the tips of her fingers, and she cast dark liquid across her blouse.

"Oh no!" Her tone made it seem like a much bigger disaster.

"Oh, Hannah. I'm so sorry," Mila consoled, looking around for anything to wipe up the mess with.

Hannah looked stricken. She leafed for a napkin in her purse and tried her best to dab out the stain, which was shaped like Africa. At that moment, Mila's name was called, and she had to wheel herself over to the front desk to meet with the rehabilitation specialist, while Hannah remained alone with her stain.

Beth Leopold greeted her warmly before wheeling her off to another section of the hospital. "I wanted to tell you, I got married a few weeks ago," Beth said brightly. "It was spontaneous, but we just decided to go for it."

"Ah! So that makes you a Montgomery, now. Congratulations! How does it feel?"

"Thank you. It feels like I'm now part of one of the biggest families on the Vineyard," Beth replied with a glint in her eye. "They're such a well-rounded family. But it also means the holidays are busy, busy, busy. And the list of presents I have to buy is very long. Not that I can complain whatsoever. The love between them all is tremendous." ."

Once within the rehabilitation clinic itself, Beth expressed sorrow that Mila would be transitioned to a different doctor for the next few months as she moved from the wheelchair to crutches back to walking again.

"Scheduling conflicts," Beth explained. "And I've moved up a bit in the department and find myself with a whole host of new duties. Beyond that..." She moved inward a bit to whisper, "I'm pregnant— I just told everyone the news."

"Oh my God. That's wonderful! Congratulations!" Mila cried as quietly as she could.

Beth blushed as though frustrated with herself for saying anything at all about herself rather than keeping focus on the patient. Still, Mila was grateful to see a human before her, rather than some doctor without a bedside manner or not an ounce of empathy. The highs and lows of life were what hospitals were all about.

"I'd like to introduce you to Jack Lawrence," Beth said as

Mila's new doctor entered the room. "He just moved to the island a few months back and recently joined us here at the hospital. He's a graduate of Harvard and a fine doctor, to boot. He's a huge fan of basketball and hockey, but he's already proven that he won't talk your ear off about sports if you ask him kindly to shut up."

Jack Lawrence was perhaps the most handsome doctor at Oak Bluffs Hospital. He was six-foot-two with eyes the color of blue ice, broad shoulders, and dark wavy blonde hair. Mila would describe him later to her best friends as, "Sort of a rugged-looking Ken doll, but the kind that comes with his own sailboat."

"Hi there," Jack greeted her with a wide smile.

For the first time since Mila's accident, Mila felt woozy with excitement. *Was this why they'd hired Jack Lawrence? To ignite her ability to live again?*

"Hi," Mila returned sheepishly.

They shook hands. Mila was conscious of the warmth of his skin and the strength of his handshake grip. Was it maybe a common thing to fall in love with the man who re-taught you how to walk? Mila had to Google that. Maybe there was a PBS documentary about it.

Beth left them after that. Jack dropped into the doctor's chair in front of her and scanned Mila's chart, which had multiple correspondences from her surgeon and other doctors.

"I've had a very extensive look at your file," Jack explained in a booming, confident voice. "That was quite an accident you had. I'm very happy to see the surgery was such a success. The doctors here are such brilliant men and women. I feel grateful to be working among them and to be a part of your health journey."

Was this a caged response, something he said to everyone who sat before him in a wheelchair? Mila's hands were suddenly clammy.

"I've outlined the next weeks and months of your journey," Jack explained as he flashed a calendar before her on the table that separated them. "I also have a ton of literature for you to read about the experience of getting your casts off, what to expect when you transition from wheelchair to crutches and back again, that kind of thing. It's important to be patient with yourself at every stage and trust your body. You're still quite young. Forty-one, correct?"

He flipped through the pages of her file. The flash of his fingers made Mila recognize that he wasn't wearing a wedding ring.

Did he have a girlfriend?

Was that an inappropriate thing to think?

Or was Mila just still reeling after Liam's abrupt departure from her life?

"Thanks for saying I'm still young at forty-one," Mila tried. "I don't always feel so young when I'm getting around the island in a wheelchair."

Jack's smile was infectious. "This is really only a temporary setback in the course of your life. You know that, don't you?"

Something about the way he said it made Mila finally believe in it. Her heart hammered against her ribcage. Perhaps a cute-man-induced heart attack was an okay thing to have at the hospital.

"And what about your support network?" Jack asked.

"My daughter and son will be home from college this weekend," Mila explained. "And my best friends have made things so easy for me. They even made a spreadsheet schedule to make sure someone's always around to, you know, get me out of bed in the morning— that kind of thing."

"You're very lucky to have so many people who love you," Jack told her firmly.

Their conversation continued for a number of minutes, with Jack taking notes about Mila's current schedule and abilities around the house. He adjusted their health schedule only slightly and told her he "looked forward" to really "getting in there" and helping her to walk again.

"You remind me of a football coach trying to get me ready for regionals," Mila joked.

"Oh yeah? I used to play football," Jack remarked as he stood up to wheel her back to the hallway.

"Figured. I know the type. I was a big-time cheerleader at Edgartown High School. It was my life," Mila told him.

"Well, look at us now," Jack replied kindly. "Football star and the cheerleader. Like nothing has ever changed."

Mila laughed. "I have a wheelchair between us that makes me think otherwise."

"Naw. That thing's only temporary, I told you. Maybe you won't do many backflips again, but you're bound to get back out there for regionals. Get your cheerleading uniform all set and ready. Deal?"

Mila knew doctors were meant to do this: boost your morale, force you to see the brightness in the midst of the darkness. But when she peered up again at those sterling blue eyes, something within her soul shifted. Jack Lawrence didn't see her as the crippled woman in the chair. Jack Lawrence saw her as a capable, beautiful forty-one-old with all the potential in the world still—en route to the rest of her life.

It was the first time she'd seen herself the way she'd longed to be seen.

Back outside, Hannah greeted her warmly, even as she spread a napkin across her coffee stain with embarrassment.

"Do you mind if we head back to my place after this?" Hannah muttered under her breath. "I feel so anxious about stains on my clothing. I always feel that the whole world is judging me."

Mila longed to tell Hannah just how little the world truly cared about a little coffee stain. The brightness of Hannah's smile was distraction enough.

Hannah drove them toward a very tiny cabin-like blue house on the edge of Edgartown, along the water line and toward the Katama Airport. Mila hadn't envisioned Hannah living along the water. In fact, it had been difficult for Mila to picture Hannah's life at all.

"Here we are," Hannah announced distractedly as she eased the car into the garage. She then blinked toward Mila as fear passed over her face like a cloud over the sun. "I suppose I should bring you inside."

Hannah said it as though she hadn't allowed anyone in her realm in many years.

"It's okay. You don't have to..." Mila replied, feeling Hannah's anxiety.

"No, no. It might take me a good while to figure out what to change into," Hannah muttered. She pulled the keys from the ignition and hustled around the back of the car, where she collected Mila's wheelchair. Mila had grown accustomed to easing from the passenger side of anyone's vehicle and onto the wheelchair, as long as it was positioned just so. Hannah seemed to intuitively understand where it needed to be.

Once around the side of Hannah's car, Mila was surprised to find a wheelchair ramp that led up from the garage floor and into the main house. Hannah eased her up the ramp and out onto the hardwood floor of her tiny abode, which was cozy and slightly cluttered, with walls that hung with countless photographs and paintings and little knickknacks from travels abroad.

When Mila glanced up toward Hannah's face, she found Hannah captivated by Mila's expression.

"What do you think?" Hannah asked softly.

"It's just so sweet in here," Mila offered with genuine affection. "Where are some of those photographs taken?"

"My husband took them overseas," Hannah recited as she headed into the little kitchenette to put on the kettle. "He had such an eye for detail. It's remarkable to see what he saw so long after the fact. We always dreamed of going to some of these places together."

Mila's heart dropped into her stomach. This was the first she'd heard of Hannah having any sort of husband.

But there, beneath a photo of the hills of France and alongside one of the Coliseums in Rome, hung a photo of two beautiful twenty-somethings— a blonde-haired, blue-eyed dream of a girl, with her arm, latched around the muscular arm of a sturdy-looking man in an army uniform.

It was clear the girl in the photograph was Hannah.

"Look at you!" Mila cried.

Hannah blushed as she hustled around the kitchen. "It was

about a million years ago. I was absolutely smitten with him. He was my soulmate. Nobody I can forget, not for a moment. I think when that man asked me to dance at the wedding, though— I think Frank blessed that wedding dance. Maybe he would want me to have a little fun, if only for old times' sake."

"I think that's very true," Mila affirmed. "I think the same about my husband sometimes. He wants me to keep living. I can feel that."

Hannah returned with two mugs of tea. With a swift motion, she removed her blouse to reveal a satin spaghetti-strap shirt beneath. Mila had never seen so much of the woman's skin before but wasn't surprised to note that it was healthy and youthful-looking, just like the rest of her. How remarkable it was to keep going when so much of your love had moved to the next life.

"What to wear? What a difficult question, and one I ask myself every day." Hannah chuckled softly as she dropped her shirt off in a little bag, which she explained she would soon take to the dry cleaners. Mila imagined Hannah owned very little that you could just wash in the washing machine.

"Do you mind if I ask..." Mila breathed as Hannah paused between the kitchen and what seemed to be her bedroom. "When Frank passed?"

Hannah's cheek twitched. "About five years ago, honey. It still feels like yesterday. He had lung cancer and was in a wheelchair for the final three years of his life. We got the hang of that thing, though. Together as a team."

Hannah then disappeared into the shadows of her bedroom in pursuit of the perfect blouse. Mila stewed in sorrow, imagining the two of them, Hannah and Frank, as they mapped out the journey of the last years of their lives together. When Mila had lost Peter, her sisters had gathered around her, creating a powerful source of support and life for Mila to lean upon. Hannah had had nothing except the leftovers of her life with Frank, including the wheelchair ramps that had made their world accessible to him.

Mila now realized how much Hannah had truly needed the job at the salon.

When Hannah stepped back out in a beautiful vintage blouse, she caught Mila's eyes glossy with tears.

"Oh, honey. I didn't mean to make you so upset with my silly house of silly memories," Hannah murmured softly.

Mila shook her head abruptly. "They're not silly. I can feel them so strongly in everything you are. The love you carry for Frank is profound, Hannah. I hope you know that. But I hope you know that there is still life to be had if you want to make it for yourself."

Hannah's eyes were heavy with doubt. "Thank you, honey. Now, can I get you some sugar for your tea?"

Chapter Sixteen

Jennifer and Mila sat at the corner of Main and School Street in downtown Edgartown as fresh and fluffy snow brushed across their noses and pink-tinged cheeks. Before them sat the bustling Edgartown Christmas Festival, a flurry of activity, of boisterous islanders mid-way through their second (or fourth) mug of mulled wine and Christmas carolers from the Edgartown Elementary school, all of whom shivered with distaste as they tried their darnedest to harmonize.

"Remember when they made us do that?" Jennifer asked with a funny laugh.

"God, yes. I was never exactly the kind of kid to do what the teachers told me. I think I was always in the back flirting with someone," Mila admitted.

"That sounds about right. Probably with Michelle, while I had to be a goody-two-shoes all the time."

Mila giggled. "Any idea what you want to eat or drink first?"

"Gosh, there's so much to choose from. We could warm our bellies with some soup? Warm our souls with some mulled wine? Suit up our sweet tooth with some Christmas cookies?"

"I like your style so far," Mila affirmed. "But I guess we'd better wait for the rest of our posse."

"Ridiculous, isn't it? They're three minutes late."

"We should really give them a warning. They'll be out of the group if they don't respect our schedules," Mila jested playfully.

"Yeah. Then it'll just be you and me, Toots. Just a couple of old ladies complaining about the world from this very corner," Jennifer quipped.

That moment, Amelia, Olivia, and Camilla bustled out from the other side of School Street, in the midst of laughter of their own. Amelia wore an oversized winter coat that fully covered her pregnant belly and dwarfed her otherwise small frame. Olivia already held a vegan hotdog aloft, saying she hadn't had time to eat that whole day and "wanted a head start." Camilla leaned over and took a bite right off of Olivia's hot dog as Olivia cried, "Hey! What do you think you're doing?" The other girls burst into giggles as Camilla chewed.

"Hey. I thought we shared everything in our little group?" Camilla's smile revealed a smudge of mustard on her lower lip.

Jennifer grabbed a clean napkin from her purse and dabbed it on Camilla's lip as she teased them all. "I don't know about you, but I'm about ready to dive in there. Mila? You ready?"

Mila saluted from her wheelchair as Camilla ambled around and gripped the handles. Lucky for them, the snow was nothing but a dusting, and the Edgartown streets had been cleaned and salted to ensure an easy wheelchair passage.

"I made a list of everything I wanted to eat," Olivia recited now. "I think we should go to this new bruschetta stand first. The guy's actually from Italy, and he makes the most divine little snacks. It'll be brain food so we can decide what we want next."

"You girls head to the bruschetta. We'll grab everyone a mug of mulled wine," Camilla affirmed before she leaned down to whisper to Mila, "I hope you don't mind? My workday was a hairy one today."

"I completely support your mulled wine mission," Mila replied.

Jennifer palled along with Mila and Camilla while Olivia and Amelia headed off to the Italian bruschetta man. Naturally, the mulled wine stand was bustling with life and a number of familiar islanders.

Audrey Sheridan held her darling nine-month-old baby, Max, in a little strap-on carrier so that his belly stretched over her chest. She stood with her cousin, Amanda Harris, along with her very pregnant Aunt Christine and her mother, Lola Sheridan. Max squawked as Camilla halted Mila's wheelchair directly beside them.

"Hi!" Christine greeted brightly as her smile curved toward her ears.

"Oh Mila, how are you feeling?" Lola swept a hand over the back of Max's carrier as her smile brightened to the strength of the surrounding Christmas lights.

"Not drunk enough for this party," Mila giggled as the Sheridan and Harris women burst into laughter.

"I feel you there," Christine offered. "Not long now before the big day."

"Good luck to you," Camilla returned. "Maybe you'll have a New Years' baby! How exciting."

"A Capricorn," Audrey added with the cluck of her tongue. "Guess that little baby will be a hard worker someday."

"Perfect. I'll retire early," Christine returned.

"Are you ladies having a good Christmas season?" Jennifer asked.

"Just about as good as ever," Lola affirmed. "Tommy, as usual, made it back to the island just barely in time for Christmas." Lola's boyfriend was an adventurous sailor who frequently left the island for wild treks across the waters. Although Lola was ordinarily incredibly upbeat about just about everything, there was occasionally a hint of sorrow in her eyes.

Jennifer wondered if Lola cursed herself for falling for the kind of man who couldn't stick around.

But she also wondered, really, if you could ever truly choose who you fell in love with.

If it had been up to Jennifer, for example, she never would have fallen out of love with Joel. It had made everything endlessly complicated.

After they grabbed mugs of mulled wine and the five servings of bruschetta, Jennifer and the girls gathered at a bench to assess the next stage of their eating strategies. There, Jennifer checked her phone again for some sign of life from Nick, who'd spent the previous several days stretched out in a heap either on her couch or in the guest bedroom.

JENNIFER: Hey, honey! I hope you're doing okay? Do you want me to grab you anything from the Festival?

She stared at her phone as the message was listed as "received."

Just after, three dots formed to prove Nick typed back. As soon as they appeared, however, the three dots disappeared. She could practically feel him becoming one with the couch all over again.

"You're texting Nick, aren't you?" Mila murmured.

Jennifer heaved a sigh. "I don't know what to do with him. Stacy's mom called me every day this week to try to discuss what to do next. I have to believe she's so dramatic that she's making Stacy feel worse about it. It's such a tragedy. Really, it is. And it tears me up inside to see them go through this. But they need each other. And they need to know that stuff like this happens all the time."

Soon after, the conversation found routes toward other avenues. Camilla reported that Andrea and Isaac would return home from their honeymoon on December 23rd, just in time for Christmas.

"You should see some of the photos they've sent me," Camilla said as she leafed for her phone. "It makes me green with envy. Here's Andrea on the beach drinking a pink cocktail. And here's Andrea on another beach drinking a green cocktail. And here's Andrea..."

"Yeah, we get it," Jennifer quipped. "I don't need to be reminded of how frozen my toes are, thank you very much."

"I hope they're bringing some of that sunshine with them?" Olivia asked.

"I don't think you can bring sunshine in a carry-on," Camilla said.

Mila lifted her chin to allow the snowflakes to plaster themselves across her forehead and cheek. "Camilla. Have you met this new doctor in the rehabilitation unit yet? Jack Lawrence?"

"Met him? No. But boy, have I heard about him."

Jennifer arched an eyebrow toward Mila, who hadn't informed any of them of this mystery person. "Jack Lawrence? Is he a movie star or something?"

Mila's cheeks burned bright red. "Beth Leopold just transferred him over to me. He gave me an outline of my 'health journey,' as he puts it, and has really good confidence that I'll be walking again by spring if you can believe it."

"That's fantastic news!" Olivia shrieked.

"Mila! Oh my God! Why didn't you tell us?" Amelia cried.

Mila shook her head but was unable to release her smile. "So, what have you heard about this Jack Lawrence guy?"

"Someone's curious about her doctor." Olivia teased.

Mila shrugged. "I just want to get a good assessment of his character."

"Well, sure. He looks like someone from the pages of a magazine," Camilla affirmed. "And word has it he's actually a damn good guy, too. He started a charity in his home city of Pittsburgh and has plans to start a branch of it here on the island."

"Why did he move here?" Mila asked.

"Someone's tone is a bit sneaky," Jennifer stated. "Why don't you ask him all this yourself?"

"Isn't it a bit inappropriate to ask your doctor too much when he's teaching you how to walk?" Mila asked.

Camilla took a long sip of wine. "As far as I can tell, he's a good guy, with a really good job and a really good heart. And... maybe this is too much to say..."

"Oh my gosh! Tell me. Whatever it is..." Mila looked about as giddy as a schoolgirl.

"Well, he's no flirt. Some of the girls have tried their darnedest to get his attention over the past few weeks, to no avail. He's committed to his work and to his patients, and he doesn't seem to want to muddy his working life with his romantic one."

Mila waved a hand to and fro. "It's not like I actually have my hopes up. I just didn't know I still had it in me to have a crush on someone, you know? And why wouldn't I have a crush on the handsome man who tells me he'll teach me how to walk again?"

"It's straight out of a romance novel," Jennifer agreed.

The Sisters' giggling conversation took them through the next few hours, as they munched through cheesy pastries and clam chowders and sizzling quesadillas, most of which they shared to allow them to have a wide palate of flavors.

Several times throughout the evening, they paused to allow Amelia to rest her aching ankles. Amelia pointed out several of the young mothers, marveling that she would soon have a little baby of her own.

"Next year, I'll have that baby strapped to my chest, just like Audrey Sheridan did," Amelia murmured. "And goodness, Mandy will have hers, too. So many new people in the world at this time next year."

Jennifer felt a strange stab of sorrow, realizing that Stacy and Nick's baby wouldn't be amongst those new humans. Their baby had had the smallest of lifespans before heading back to heaven.

Amelia seemed to sense this shift in Jennifer. She reached over and spread a hand over Jennifer's shoulder. No words were necessary.

"This time next year, I won't be able to sit still," Mila told them excitedly. "You won't see me sitting on any bench whatsoever. I'll run marathons and go back to dance class and work on my high-kicks all over again, like my cheerleading days."

"Uh oh. Mila's devolving into a teenager," Jennifer teased.

"And I love it!" Camilla cried.

Mila laughed playfully. "Isabelle and Zane are having a fun time whipping me around the house now that they're home. I swear Zane's rough housing is going to wind me up in the hospital again. But their laughter is infectious. I feel younger now than I did a few months ago. And to be honest?"

The girls leaned in closer for this bit of juicy information.

"I realized I don't miss Liam at all," Mila confided. "He was such a wonderful small part of my newly-widowed timeline. Maybe he reminded me that I was deserving of something bigger than what I thought. Now that I've seen Hannah's lonely reality, I know that you should fight for what you want your life to be, no matter what. I don't want loneliness. I want laughter. I want love. I want to run and jump and play."

In the distance, the carolers began a soft, lilting version of "Silent Night." It felt as though it came from a dream.

"I don't know where any of this is going, and for the first time, I'm kind of glad," Mila told them now.

"Well, I know where we should head next," Olivia finally advised after a long pause. "I saw a cheese stand with about twelve different French cheeses we've never tried before. Who's in?"

The Sisters' laughter followed Olivia as she raced off to nab a wide selection of fatty, salty delights. Jennifer squeezed Mila's shoulder warmly as Mila shared her infectious smile. For just a moment, after the chaos of the past few weeks, everything felt just as it always had before.

Chapter Seventeen

Isabelle shifted and yanked herself over so that the bed beneath Mila shook. Mila's eyes scanned the curve of Isabelle's cheek, all she could see in the soft grey light of this December 22nd morning. It was three days till Christmas and the third day in a row that Isabelle had fallen asleep alongside her mother, as though she was a much younger girl struggling with nightmares. Perhaps Isabelle was old enough, now, to uncover the truth: that nightmares were entirely real, the stuff of the every day, and you had to force yourself to hover above them with laughter and love and hope; otherwise, the darkness took over.

When Isabelle awoke twenty-five minutes later, she rolled into her mother and placed her head on her shoulder. She smelled of yesterday's makeup and yesterday's perfume, despite Mila telling her time and time again to cleanse and moisturize. Now wasn't the time for that lecture.

"You want to get up, Momma?" Isabelle breathed.

Isabelle was already a master at the move-Mila-from-bed-to-wheelchair situation, so much so that she easily gossiped as she did it. Once Mila was safely in the bathroom, Isabelle remained outside the door, running her mouth into an endless stream of creativity and facts. She'd recently broken up with another boy at school, a Chemistry major, and now struggled with seeing his social media updates, as he was vacationing in Hawaii for the holidays and she was "aching with jealousy."

When Mila wheeled herself out of the bathroom, she teased Isabelle with, "But didn't you say he was about the most boring guy you've ever met in your life?"

Isabelle grumbled. "Yes. But I could make peace with boring if he took me to Hawaii for Christmas every year."

Isabelle followed after Mila as Mila wheeled herself into the kitchen. Isabelle flashed through the Chem-major's social media updates for Mila to see while Mila poured coffee grounds into a filter and blinked bleary eyes.

"See? He looks great. Six pack abs, Mom! Am I being stupid?"

"Honey, there are so many men in the world," Mila told her. "If this one bored you, you deserve to find someone who doesn't."

"Is she still complaining about Chem-Major?" Zane stepped out of the shadowy hallway in a pair of pajama pants and nothing else. He scratched his hairy chest as he hunted through the fridge for something to eat.

"Whatever, Zane. Not like you ever make yourself emotionally vulnerable enough to fall for anyone." Isabelle flipped her long tresses down her back.

Zane stuck out his tongue as he rustled cereal into a bowl.

"You're both nineteen years old. I think you have some time before you make any big decisions about your romantic future," Mila countered playfully.

"Nineteen and getting older every day," Isabelle breathed dramatically.

"Oh my gosh..." Zane rolled his eyes as he snapped the top off the container of almond milk.

Mila hung around the house with Isabelle and Zane as they snacked on Christmas cookies, watched silly Christmas movies, played board games (all of which inevitably made Zane "bored out of his mind"), and teased each other. Toward the end of the afternoon, Isabelle and Zane showered and dressed to meet friends, as was their custom.

"I know. It's so lame hanging around here with your mom," Mila shot, only partly joking.

"Whatever, Mom. We just have to make ourselves seen on the island, you know?" Zane countered.

"Yeah. We aren't here all the time, but we can't let anyone forget about us just in case we come back," Isabelle said.

Mila laughed. "I hope that means you're coming back?"

"For the summer for sure," Zane affirmed. "I wouldn't know what to do with myself anywhere else."

With her kids out of the house, Mila piled onto the couch and stretched her cast-legs out. Within the next month, the casts would be removed and she would be allowed to see her legs again. This filled her with a strange sense of fear. Would they be lined with scars? Unrecognizable? She knew she was meant to appreciate every stage of her journey, but occasionally, she hit a hiccup.

Jennifer texted to ask what was up. Mila invited her over for

"snacks and a Christmas movie since my kids decided I'm too lame to hang out with." Jennifer agreed and arrived at Mila's place on Witchwood twenty minutes later, armed with a bottle of wine and everything to fill her chartreuse board, including various cheeses, pickles, various meats, and condiments.

"Look! Do you remember this Christmas movie?" Mila gestured toward the screen. "The Family Stone with Sarah Jessica Parker?"

"I think I really liked this one." Jennifer churned the cork out from within the bottle of wine and poured them two hearty glasses. "She's really uptight and dating Luke Wilson?"

"That's it," Mila confirmed. "Here. I think I can rewind it actually."

"Newfangled technology," Jennifer said, impressed.

"Isabelle made me realize I've been using our smart TV all wrong," Mila told her. "It feels like I didn't maximize all my days at home, but hey— I did manage to get through that whole stack of books." Mila pointed toward a stack of fifteen novels, most of which involved romance in some capacity. She couldn't help it. She was a sucker.

As the opening credits rolled on *The Family Stone*, Jennifer cleared her throat and said, "Listen. I heard a rumor about Liam, and Amelia just confirmed it. You know, she knows what's-what and who's-who around Edgartown."

Mila's heart stopped beating for a split second. "Okay. I want to know."

"He took some time off the police force and is staying with family off the island," Jennifer explained.

Mila nodded. Her eyes filled with tears. She blinked several times so that they would not fall.

"I sometimes wonder if I should reach out to him. Try to tell him how okay it is that we're no longer in contact," Mila murmured.

"I don't think it's your job to make things easier on him," Jennifer said. "He hurt you, and in the process, he hurt himself. It all seems so useless to me."

Mila held the silence for a long moment. Her heart remembered its old crackly nature and seemed to ache with old wounds. Just as she opened her lips to speak, however, her phone rang. It was Hannah.

"I have to get this, but I won't be long," Mila explained to Jennifer. "Hannah! Hi. Merry Christmas."

For a long moment, the other line was filled only with silence. Mila's eyebrows crinkled together.

"Hannah?"

Jennifer's face was difficult to read. She mouthed, "Did she butt dial you?"

But just then, Hannah spoke in a meek tone.

"Mila. Mila... I made a horrible mistake."

Mila's heart quickened. "Hannah? What happened? What mistake?"

Jennifer snapped upright on the cushioned chair. She reached for her purse on instinct, ready for whatever.

"I... I did something awful," Hannah whispered as her voice cracked. "I don't know if I can take it back."

Mila waved a hand wildly toward her wheelchair, trying to express to Jennifer just how quickly they needed to move.

"What did you do, Hannah? Just tell me, and we can fix it together."

"Mila, I took so many... so many pills."

Mila clenched her eyes tight. Jennifer positioned the wheelchair alongside the couch so that Mila could easily slip inside. Mila stuttered with her answer.

"I'm going to call 9-1-1, Hannah, okay? Just sit where you are. I'll meet you up at the hospital. Do you hear me?"

Jennifer hurriedly grabbed her phone and dialed 9-1-1 instead. When she had the operator, Mila muttered Hannah's address so that Jennifer could pass the information on. "She swallowed too many pills," she whispered as Jennifer's eyes widened.

"Are you still there, Hannah?" Mila asked, trying to make her voice sound soothing and calm.

"What?" Hannah sounded terribly confused and far away.

Jennifer donned her winter coat and wheeled Mila out to her car, where she helped her onto the passenger seat. All the while, Hannah mumbled nothingness into the phone as Mila tried to keep her conscious. After another few minutes, there was the blare of the sirens as the ambulance arrived outside Hannah's place.

"I'm going to let you go, Hannah, okay? The men there will help you. And we'll see you at the hospital. Okay? Okay?"

But Hannah seemed no longer able to answer. There was a horrible crashing sound as the EMT workers broke through the door to get to Hannah. Hannah's confused shriek erupted through the phone. After a long moment, someone seemed to take Hannah's cell and end the call.

"Oh my God," Jennifer whispered.

"I knew she was lonely..." Mila began. "God, why didn't I see that she was also..."

"It's okay. You can't blame yourself for this," Jennifer tried to comfort her. "I'm just so grateful she reached out to you to tell you what she'd done. It could have gone very differently."

Mila and Jennifer drove in stunned silence. It was now such a familiar route, this trek from Edgartown to the Oak Bluffs Hospital. Once outside the emergency room, Jennifer texted Camilla to see if she was on duty. Luckily, she was and hustled out to greet them in the waiting room between her duties.

"They have Hannah here already," she murmured as she smeared a hand over her sweat-lined forehead. "And they're pumping her stomach."

"Gosh..." Mila dropped her chin to her chest as Camilla rubbed her shoulder distractedly.

"They think it was her husband's old medicine," Camilla murmured. "Stuff she still had on-hand after he died."

"How much longer till we know if she's..." Jennifer began.

Camilla shook her head. "She'll probably be unconscious for a few hours. I'll know more around nine or ten. You two could even head home. I'll call you when she wakes up."

But Mila protested this idea. "I can't go, Jen. You can if you want to. But Hannah doesn't have any family on the island. She's allowed me a small part of her world for some reason, and I can't squander that."

"I understand."

Jennifer and Mila perched in the corner of the emergency waiting room. Jennifer flipped through a fashion magazine while Mila stared into space. She often wondered about the hours her friends had waited just outside as she'd been unconscious on the operating table. What had run through their minds? Had they thought she would die?

How lucky Mila was to have lived through such a horrible event. Being back in the emergency room was a real reminder of that. She needed to learn to count her blessings each and every day.

After Camilla found another break in her schedule, she burst through the double-wide doors to report that Hannah's stomach had been successfully pumped and she was "resting peacefully."

"She's been moved to another wing of the hospital," Camilla explained. "But visiting hours are over, I'm afraid. You'll have to come back tomorrow morning first thing."

This wasn't good enough for Mila.

"I don't know. Is there a way you can just wheel me in? I practically look like a patient," she protested.

"Mila, I mean, I would. But shouldn't you get some rest tonight? My primary concern is your health, to be honest," Camilla countered.

"I'm mostly fine," Mila offered.

"Tell that to the casts on your legs," Camilla replied curtly.

"Come on. I don't want Hannah to wake up confused about where she is," Mila blared. "It's really crazy. She wanted to leave the world today. I want her to wake up and be grateful that she didn't."

Camilla sighed before she glanced back toward the hallway, which swarmed with beeping sounds and lights and frantic activity. "I can get you in through another entrance if you drive around. But just for the record, I'm not too pleased with the idea."

"Jen. You in?" Mila asked, looking up at her from her wheelchair.

Jennifer grumbled as she stretched her arms over her head. "Who doesn't love a night in the hospital? As far as I'm concerned, it's the best hotel in town."

Chapter Eighteen

Mila awoke abruptly at the crack of dawn to find sixty-four-year-old Hannah's bright blue eyes peering at her through the grey light. Mila's lips crept into a smile. "Good morning, beautiful," Mila murmured as she stretched her arms above her head.

Hannah's voice was groggy and far away, as though it came from another dimension. "What are you doing here?"

Mila wheeled herself closer to Hannah's bed. She cast a glance to the right, where Jennifer had stretched herself over two chairs and slumbered with her vibrant red curls cast over her double-folded coat.

"We were waiting for you to wake up," Mila explained gently. She brought a hand over Hannah's tenderly, remembering that first afternoon when Hannah had come to visit her in the hospital. How confused Mila had been to see her.

Hannah's once-perfect hair had frizzed against the hospital

pillow. Her makeup had mussed to reveal a slightly older facade, one she assuredly didn't want the rest of the world to see. Hannah lifted her fingers to her forehead and whispered, "I have a hunch I don't look my best."

"You shouldn't think about that," Mila tried before laughing quietly. "Although who am I to tell a beauty queen like Hannah what she's meant to feel?"

Hannah's cheeks flushed crimson. Her blue eyes moved toward the beeping machine she was hooked up to. Minute-by-minute, she seemed to connect the dots of what she'd done. Shame reflected in her eyes.

"I can't believe myself," she whispered.

"You shouldn't think that way." Mila's voice was stern but kind.

"I'm used to the grey. It's been that way since my husband passed. My moods are low, but I can deal with them. I carry them with me. But last night, I caught a Christmas special on the television, one of those silly ones about families coming together. An older couple welcomed their daughter after years and years apart. It tore into me. We— we couldn't have children. I couldn't, and we always said we were happier without them, that we were enough. And we were until he passed on and left me in that house alone."

Hannah squeezed her eyes shut. Her coloring shifted toward grey. Mila squeezed her hand gently, wanting to keep her in the light of the new day a moment longer.

"I just feel so tired," Hannah admitted then. "I think I'd like to rest a bit longer."

"Keep sleeping," Mila offered. "I'll be around, okay?"

Hannah nodded while her eyes remained closed. "Mila, I'm so glad you're here."

After Hannah slipped off to sleep again, Jennifer awoke. Mila whispered what had happened with Hannah, and Jennifer nodded sadly. "I think you're right. She needed you here when she woke up. Just knowing someone else in the world cares about her..."

Mila's eyes felt terribly heavy. Jennifer lifted her arms over her head as a yawn stretched her face. "Ooph. I smell terrible," she blurted before she tilted her head toward the hall and continued, "What do you say we run to the bathroom for a little wash-up before I head home and say hi to my son?"

Once in the hospital bathroom, the girls removed their shirts, scrubbed their armpits, and tousled their hair. Jennifer smeared moisturizer across her cheeks and forehead before passing it over to Mila, who scoffed at the brand before saying, "I gave you that other bottle for your birthday! Where is it?"

Jennifer rolled her eyes. "Mila, I don't keep every bottle of moisturizer on me at all times."

Mila laughed. "Well, I do." She hunted through her purse, through her wide array of eyebrow pencils and eyeliners, mascaras, moisturizers, and concealers. Jennifer grumbled that she was a walking esthetician salon— something Mila thanked her for with a funny wink before she finished up her own makeup. When she leaned back to take in full view of herself, she laughed outright.

"We don't look like we slept in a hospital all night."

"The volume of our hair is pretty ridiculous, though. Like we're groupies for a rock band," Jennifer joked. "And at forty-two, I certainly feel like I slept at a hospital."

Mila gripped her hand. "Thank you again. It really meant the world to me that you stuck around."

"Don't mention it, Mil. I know you'd do the same for me."

With Jennifer gone for a bit, Mila roamed the nearly empty halls of the hospital on the hunt for a cup of coffee and a charging station for her cell phone. She planned to spend the day with Hannah and hoped, even, to be there upon her release. According to texts from Isabelle and Zane, both were "a bit hungover" and would probably sleep through the day, anyway.

MILA: My lazy, lazy children.

ISABELLE: We love you!

ZANE: Ly.

When Mila lifted her eyes from her cell, she found a very familiar face before her.

Her rehabilitation doctor, Jack Lawrence, stood in his hospital whites with his thick arms crossed over his chest. He looked like a high school principal about to announce that Mila had gotten into trouble yet again.

"Well, well, well. Someone can't stay away from the hospital," he jested with a grin.

Mila matched his infectious smile. She slipped her phone back in her purse and thanked the heavens and the stars above that she'd done her makeup and hair only ten minutes before.

"No way. Night and day, I'm here," Mila returned.

"What is it about this place that you like so much? It can't be the food or the coffee."

Mila laughed. "Obviously, it's men like you who boss me around."

"Ah. So that's your thing," he countered.

"If I have to have a thing, maybe that's it," Mila said.

"Nobody has to have a thing. It's just a bit easier to categorize everyone."

Mila eyed him for a second. "I don't think I'm so easily categorized. Not since the cheerleading days, anyway."

Jack's smile fell the slightest bit. A beat passed between them. Mila was reminded of her deceased husband, Peter, and how he'd been able to just glance her way and know exactly what she was thinking.

"You're not here for a good reason, though. Are you?"

Mila shook her head as her flirtatious smile fell from her lips. "It's all okay now. A friend had an accident."

"I'm so sorry." Mila could tell from his tone that he really meant it. He dropped his hands on either side of his frame as he said, "Is there anything I can do?"

Mila shook her head. "No. I'm just trying to be there for her in any way I can. She doesn't have any family around here to speak of and not many friends, either."

Jack's eyes dropped to the ground. "You know, I just read a report about all the people across the United States who are left alone over the holidays. It breaks my heart to think about it. I've never faced loneliness in that way. Of course, I've had a dark month here and there."

"Who hasn't?" Mila murmured.

"But I can't imagine that. The years going by as the rest of the world moves on without you," Jack said softly.

Mila's heart shattered. Again, a beat of silence passed between them.

"Do you have Christmas plans?" she asked him.

Jack nodded. "I'm from Pittsburgh. I'm headed there this afternoon after I finish my shift. My mom always makes a ham and we eat ourselves silly throughout Christmas Eve and Christmas. I also have, get this, six brothers and sisters."

"No!" Mila laughed until her stomach quaked. "You must have had the loudest house imaginable."

"No loneliness around there," Jack agreed. "And I sometimes miss how chaotic it was, especially with how quiet my little bachelor pad is these days."

Bachelor. He'd purposefully told her he was a bachelor.

"Well, I'd better get back to my friend," Mila said hurriedly.

"Yes, and I have a client. But it was good to see you, Mila. I guess we have our next appointment on..."

"The twenty-eighth," Mila affirmed.

"Right before the New Year," he said excitedly. "And like I said before. We'll have you out of that chair by spring."

Mila's excitement mounted. "I hope you're right about that."

"I'm no liar, Mila," Jack told her as his blue eyes widened. "You have to trust me as we go through this process together. I'm looking so forward to it."

"Me too."

When Mila returned to Hannah's room, she found Camilla in the doorway. Little shadows rounded beneath Camilla's eyes as she greeted Mila with a big hug.

"How's she doing?"

"She woke up a little while ago," Mila explained. "I think I'm going to ask her to come to stay with us at the house. Nobody should be alone on Christmas."

"Nobody should be alone ever," Camilla corrected.

"All right, know-it-all," Mila quipped as her eyes filled with tears. "Sorry. It's been a weird twelve hours."

"I understand. Everything's making me cry right now. Andrea's headed home today and I think I might burst into tears when I see her. My baby girl! All grown up and married!"

"Will you all make it to Jennifer's for Christmas?" Mila asked.

"Yes. For sure," Camilla assured her as she dotted the edge of her sleeve across her tear-filled eyes. "We never miss it."

Mila wheeled back into Hannah's room. As she waited for Hannah to awake again, she dozed off, herself, and fell into a dream state of her own, all of which involved Peter and the sailboat he'd once loved to sail. He stretched his broad hand out toward her as his booming voice asked, *"What do you say, Mila? You want to sail the seven seas?"*

A nurse's voice awoke Mila twenty-five minutes later. She asked Hannah about her pain levels and informed her the doctor would be in soon. She also said that she would be assigned a psychologist for the foreseeable future. Hannah thanked her timidly, as though she was embarrassed. Mila wanted to tell her not to be— that sometimes, the weight of life was just too much to carry on your own.

Hannah was slightly brighter now that she'd slept a few hours more. She gestured toward her face and said, "I don't know what to do with myself. I never go out in public like this."

Mila laughed, remembering what Jennifer had said about her purse. "Lucky for you, I'm a walking esthetician salon," she said as she slung the bag up onto the bed for Hannah to see.

Mila propped up a hand mirror for the next half hour while Hannah performed a duty Mila understood in her very soul. Self-care was essential. It was a conversation you had with yourself to affirm your own self-worth. It wasn't just about how the world saw you; it was also how you saw yourself.

When Hannah finished, she leaned back to assess her reflection.

"How funny. After all that work, I'm still sixty-four years old." Hannah tried out a joke.

Mila remembered her own assumption that humor would make her injuries easier to handle, even as Amelia had scolded her.

"Unfortunately, time travel makeup hasn't been invented yet," Mila told her.

"Well, they had better get around to it," Hannah returned. "Because I will pay top dollar for it."

Mila laughed. "What age do you think is the best age to be?"

Hannah shifted her hand over her stomach. "I don't know. How old are you?"

"I'm not the perfect age," Mila insisted.

"Maybe the perfect age is just whatever you're not at the time," Hannah offered thoughtfully. "You experience everything a few years later anyway, right?"

"I think that's unfortunately true, no matter how hard I try to live in the moment."

Hannah allowed a single tear to trace down her cheek. Mila wasn't sure how to take the pain from her heart.

"I hate these hospital gowns," Hannah confessed instead, which made Mila burst into laughter.

"I hate them, too. So much," she admitted. "When I left the hospital, I wanted to burn mine."

Hannah formed her first genuine smile of the day. After a

moment of silence, Mila told her, with finality, what would happen next.

"I want you to come to stay with me for a little while. I promise I won't get in the way of your schedule, and we can move your entire beautiful wardrobe along with you. But there's no reason you should be in that house alone around Christmas time. I won't hear of it."

Hannah looked as though she wanted to protest. She swallowed the lump in her throat and turned her blue eyes toward the ceiling. Before she could speak, however, Mila offered up one more thing.

"My daughter and son are both home from college. Together, we'll be like a big, wild, happy family. It'll be loud, but it'll be home."

Hannah's eyes glittered with a mix of sorrow and intrigue.

"It sounds..."

"Chaotic? Loud?" Mila tried.

"No. It sounds like what Christmas is supposed to be," Hannah murmured instead. "I'd love to stay, if only for a little while."

Chapter Nineteen

Jennifer sat half-awake on the cushy couch in her and Derek's condominium living room as soft snow shifted out from the grey clouds above. Her eyes were only slits, her vision bleary. Derek stepped out of the kitchen in a pair of high socks, flannel pajama bottoms, and a white T. He passed a mug of coffee to Jen before he dropped a kiss on her cheek and whispered, "You're just so kind to your friends. I aspire to your kindness."

"Not overly kind," Jen corrected. "I just love them to pieces is all and that poor woman..." She shook her head as she outlined more of what had happened with Hannah the previous evening. "Mila conned Camilla into getting us into her hospital room."

"Sounds like Mila," Derek replied with the slightest of smiles.

Jennifer sipped her coffee, which was almost as good as the coffee Joel had made her for years on end. Almost.

"You're getting better about them, aren't you?" she asked Derek now.

"What do you mean?"

"My best friends. You know them. You know their little intricacies and their senses of humor."

Derek gave a little shrug before he collapsed on the couch beside her. "To know you and to love you is to love your friends. If I hadn't caught on to all of that, I have a hunch you would have kicked me to the curb by now."

Jennifer massaged his upper back lovingly. "You know what? I think you're right about that," she teased.

Derek burst into laughter at that. His smile echoed back all the love he felt for her. Just before he leaned in to kiss her, however, Nick jumped out of the guest room in a pair of basketball shorts and an old t-shirt from high school. His dark curls were untamed and mangy, and his eyes were blood-tinged.

"Honey, what's wrong? What happened?" Jennifer demanded, half-panicked.

"Stacy agreed to go for a walk," he explained, as though he'd just announced he planned to run for president. He stopped short at the end of the hallway and ran his fingers through his hair. "I don't know... I don't know what to do. She hasn't let me see her since it all happened."

Jennifer placed her mug of coffee on the side table and stood up to hug her son. Even into his twenties, he still had these moments of deep, impenetrable fears. Jennifer knew well that those fears never really went away.

"Honey, you'll just do what you've always done," she whispered to him as she hugged him close. "You'll love each other, and you'll find a way through this— together."

With Nick in the shower (his first in what seemed like many

days), Jennifer draped her head over Derek's chest and allowed her eyes to close. What seemed like a split-second later, she opened her eyes to the vision of a fully-cleaned-up, well-dressed Nick, the one reminiscent of the young man who'd just married the love of his life.

"Buy her flowers on the way," Jennifer said sleepily.

"Oh. Great idea," Nick affirmed.

"The Oak Bluffs flower shop. Claire..." Jennifer continued.

"Right. Of course. Of course." Nick dropped down and kissed Jen on the cheek before he headed for the day. "See you later, Derek."

"Good luck, man."

After the door clicked closed, Jennifer rolled off of Derek and realized, with a funny jolt of her gut, that she'd drooled all over Derek's white T. She scrunched her nose with embarrassment. Was she allowed to drool on this man so soon after the beginning of their still-new relationship?

Derek's eyes glowed with happiness. He seemed to not notice nor care about the drool.

"I think those kids will be okay," he said then as they shared a smile. After a long pause, he added, "Feels like I haven't seen you one-on-one in a little while."

"It's been a busy time," Jennifer agreed.

"What do you say we head out for a walk of our own? We can bundle up and grab some coffee and walk along the bay."

"Sounds romantic," Jennifer teased.

"That was the idea, yeah," Derek teased right back.

Jennifer inspected herself in the mirror to find that her makeup job at the hospital was still pretty well intact. She suggested she shower before they headed out, but Derek insisted that they "shower later, together" after the walk. Jennifer's heart ballooned. How had she gotten so lucky to have this second version of love?

They headed out into the flurries of snow with their gloved hands latched around each other. The snow-flecked across Derek's hair and made him look more salt-and-pepper than he already was. Jennifer wondered if they'd one day grow old together— or if this was just a temporary thing, as fleeting as the snow that shimmered down and melted on the cement.

Oh, but it wasn't time to ask such questions. It was time to enjoy the splendor of this day, just two days before Christmas.

"Emma should get in this evening," Derek told her as they neared the crosswalk. "I hope that bracelet is enough for her present?"

"I picked up a journal and a few books as well," Jennifer said. "I noticed she was a big reader last time she was here."

"She's really taken that on lately," Derek said proudly. "But it's amazing you noticed that."

"I'm a woman. It's our job to notice these things."

"I've been lucky to be surrounded by beautiful, kind, and considerate women my whole life-long. I don't know what I did right, but I'm grateful."

They continued to walk: through downtown and then onward toward the docks, which were now cleared of most of the summer season's boats. They grabbed two cups of coffee from a nearby vendor and stepped out onto the creaking boards. The Edgartown Lighthouse stood so domineering before them, a reminder of long-lost days of adventurous sailors and whalers, an era the island had lost.

Out on the edge of the dock, Derek kissed her tenderly, placing his hand across her cheek and his other across the small of her back. Jennifer's knees threatened to give out, as though she was a young woman in a Regency novel and not the forty-two-year-old divorcee she actually was. How easy it was, sometimes, to fall into a daydream.

When they stepped off the dock a few minutes later, Jennifer stopped short at a familiar sight along the boardwalk.

There before them, dressed in a thick dark green winter coat she'd purchased on sale several years before, was her ex-husband, Joel. His eyes widened with surprise. Derek stepped up beside her, noticed Joel, and halted as well. It felt like a stand-off, like they were a car and Joel was a moose in their way.

"Hi!" Jennifer greeted him brightly.

"Hi there."

Joel stepped toward her and Jennifer gave him a less-than-passionate hug, as she didn't want to get too into it in front of Derek. It felt cold when compared to the life they'd lived together. Immediately afterward, Joel and Derek shook hands.

"What are you doing out here?" Jennifer asked, trying to keep the energy up.

"Just out for a walk. Wanted to see the snow," Joel replied, hands shoved deep in his pockets.

"Same." Jennifer twirled a strand of red hair around her ear and felt the weight of time between them. How many walks had she and Joel shared in the rain, sleet, snow, and sun? Hundreds, if not thousands, maybe. How strange that they probably wouldn't walk together again, not in the same way. She also remembered the rumor that he and Renée had broken up recently. Was she rubbing her new relationship in his face?

"Nick's with Stacy right now," Jennifer finally added. "They're going to try to patch things up."

"Gosh, that's good to hear," Joel said. "Nick's been so unresponsive to my text messages and calls this week."

"He hasn't been responsive to us, either, from inside the guest room," Jennifer countered.

Joel's eyes turned toward Derek, echoing the strangeness of the situation. Probably, it was difficult for Joel to know that Derek had had more access to his grieving son than he'd had.

"Well, I hope you'll tell him I said hi," Joel finally added.

Jennifer's eyes filled with tears just then. "Of course. I'm sure he'll call you."

"Sure." Joel adjusted his dark yellow winter cap. "By the way, maybe you heard, but me and Renée broke up."

"That's really too bad, Joel. I'm really sorry to hear that. I liked her."

"Yeah. I did, too." Joel shoved both hands into his pockets again. "Well, I'd better keep walking. Lots of Christmas cookies to eat over the next few days. My mom went a little wild with it this year."

"Right. Well. Hope to see you around soon," Jennifer said.

With Joel far down the boardwalk and Jennifer and Derek headed in the opposite direction, Jennifer felt a strange coldness stretch over her stomach. She squeezed harder on Derek's hand without fully realizing it until he stopped short yet again and turned his eyes toward hers.

"Jennifer. Can I ask you a question?"

Jennifer's lips parted in surprise. "Of course. Anything."

Derek stuttered at first. "I'm sure this has all been a whirlwind for you. Selling the house, you had with him and Nick. Ending your marriage and moving in with me. And I just have to be sure because I've heard stories about you and Joel ever since I met you. You don't want to get back together with him. Do you?"

Jennifer was surprised that Derek had sensed any hesitation within her at all. She'd expected that she'd hidden it well enough, in a dark, shadowy place within her soul.

But Derek was better than to be lied to.

"It's been a whirlwind," Jennifer agreed. "And to be honest with you, sometimes I feel very, very sad that my marriage fell apart."

Derek's face didn't fidget. He seemed to have expected this somehow and prepared for the worst.

"But my sorrow over my marriage has nothing to do with you or with us," she continued. "You've given me something to hope for. You've taught me that things can grow and change, that sometimes what life gives you isn't what you expected. Sometimes, what life gives you is even better than what you planned for."

Derek's eyes watered with tears. "Thank you for being honest with me."

"I love you, Derek. I really do. You're beyond this island girl's wildest dreams. I just wish— I wish sometimes you were linked to those other parts of my life that I loved so much."

"Like your sister," Derek murmured.

"Yes. But I know you've lost people you've loved— your wife. I can only imagine what you felt for her. I can only imagine what it was like to lose her. And I feel so grateful that you've allowed space in your heart for me."

They held one another's gaze for a long moment. Derek's thumb traced a line over her cheek. He seemed captivated by her. But just before he dropped his head over hers for a kiss, he twitched his eyes over in such a way that Jennifer was forced to turn around to see what had grabbed him.

Two blocks away, seated on a bench as the snow floated down around them, were Nick and Stacy.

Stacy's forehead was pressed against Nick's chest as her little frame shook against him. His sturdy hand-stretched over her back as he held her tightly against him. He was her calm in the midst of a horrible storm. Now, he was allowed to do what he'd wanted to do since the miscarriage had happened.

"Look at them," Jennifer whispered. "They have all they need."

Derek wrapped his arm around her shoulder and held her tightly as they took in the view of the young married couple. Jennifer's heart swelled with love for them.

"I hope you know I'll be there for you through thick and thin, too," Derek murmured. "Whatever life throws at us. We can handle it. Together."

Chapter Twenty

Every Christmas, Jennifer's dearest friends (and their families) gathered at Jennifer's parents' home for a Christmas celebration that spun with endless laughter, platters and platters of sinfully delicious food, perfectly shiny wrapped presents, and hours and hours of conversation and feigned arguments and squabbles. The tradition had begun around the time of Michelle's death, as the other Sisters of Edgartown's family had ached with such sorrow over their loss that they'd wanted to hold one another up in any way they could. Michelle was gone; she wouldn't ever return. But they had enough love to keep one another going, for now.

Ariane, Jennifer, and Stacy stood in the kitchen during the mid-morning on Christmas as snow swirled out from the sky above. Soft Christmas jazz buzzed from Ariane's speakers as she made her way around the kitchen in a half-dance. Just the previous year, she'd hardly been able to walk from the kitchen to the living room. *My, what changes a year brought*, Jennifer thought now.

Just after Ariane danced into the foyer, she called out, "I think Camilla's here!"

Jennifer hustled past the television, where Derek, her father, John, and her son, Nick, sat with mugs of coffee, captivated with whatever sporting event had recently happened. Jennifer flung open the front door to find Camilla, Jonathon, Andrea, and Isaac pop out of Camilla's car and speed through the snow to greet her. True to what Camilla had suggested, Andrea and Isaac were both tanned beauties after their honeymoon, and Jennifer screeched with jealousy as she hugged Andrea close.

"There's our fashion school grad," she teased. "How was Hawaii?"

"Oh, it was just okay..." Andrea said sarcastically.

"Oh, please," Jennifer returned with a laugh. "Get in there and grab a freshly-baked donut. Me and Mom woke up early to make a specialty batch."

"If there's anything the Conrad women know, it's donuts," Camilla shot with a laugh.

Just before Jennifer could duck inside and out of the cold, Olivia, Anthony, Chelsea, and Xavier arrived in Anthony's huge work truck. Chelsea had recently dyed her hair hot pink, which suited her, strangely, and probably made her just-another-hip-girl in Brooklyn.

"Your mom is going to freak when she sees Chelsea's hair, isn't she?" Olivia asked as she hugged Jennifer close.

"You know Ariane. She's shocked about today's fashions," Jennifer said. "But she'll survive. It's just hair."

Xavier looked jittery and strange as he walked into the house after Chelsea. They were a rather new item, as they'd just paired up at the beginning of the year after Olivia had received The Hesson House from her Great Aunt. At the time, Xavier had been a borderline "bad kid" before finding common ground with Chelsea and building what seemed to be an honest and beautiful romance.

Jennifer hopped inside to check on Christmas dinner, which Stacy and Ariane had under control. Just as Jennifer poured herself another mug of coffee, the door cracked open again to reveal Hannah, Isabelle, Zane, and Mila.

"Thank you for putting that wheelchair ramp up outside," Mila said brightly as she greeted Jennifer. "I brought my three servants with me. I hope you don't mind."

Hannah was dressed in her Christmas best: a bright-as-ruby-red dress with a green scarf and dangling pearl earrings. Her hair gleamed beautifully, as bright as the snow outside, and she greeted Jennifer with a timid yet warm voice. "Thank you so much for welcoming me into your home."

Isabelle flounced into the house and headed straight for Chelsea. "I love your hair. Tell me all about Brooklyn." She landed cross-legged in front of Xavier and Isabelle, rapt with attention.

Mila rolled her eyes playfully as she wheeled into the kitchen. "Tell me how I can help."

"I guess we're just waiting on Amelia?" Ariane asked as she placed her hands on her hips.

"She's normally the only one ever on time," Olivia teased.

"It's still too early for her..." Ariane began, speaking of her potential childbirth.

"Yes. Too early," Jennifer confirmed. "Wouldn't be a good thing."

"Ah! There she is." Camilla called from the front window.

Together, Camilla, Mila, Olivia, and Jennifer hustled into the foyer to greet Amelia, her niece, Mandy, who was about an inch more pregnant than Amelia, plus Oliver, Amelia's boyfriend, into the fold. Isabelle, who'd been friendly with Mandy during their high school days, rushed into the foyer to ogle Mandy's baby belly. "You're simply gorg, Mandy," she gushed.

"Are we saying 'gorg' now?" Jennifer asked.

"You're not," Isabelle teased.

"Ah. I guess we can't say certain things after the age of forty?" Mila tried.

"I don't make the rules," Isabelle quipped as she tossed her hair.

The natural order of things led Chelsea, Isabelle, Mandy, Andrea, and Stacy to the dining room table for a glass of wine and a bout of twenty-something conversation while the forty-something women lingered in the kitchen. Zane and Nick swapped old sports stories from their days on the field while the other men watched the television with rapt attention. Hannah began a conversation with Ariane about Ariane's beautiful china collection, which she hardly touched since they'd belonged to her own mother.

"Oh, but shouldn't we use them today?" Hannah tried. "They're too beautiful to be kept on a shelf."

Ariane considered this thoughtfully. "You might have a point there, Hannah. How else am I meant to enjoy them? My mother would have wanted them to be used."

Jennifer turned toward Mila, whom she hadn't seen since their stint at the hospital a few nights before.

"How's it been at your place?"

Mila's smile was electric. "Hannah, Isabelle, and I created a spa day for ourselves yesterday. We listened to music and did facials and painted our nails." She flashed her fingers around to show a deep burgundy. "We tried to get Zane into it, but he resisted everything but the snacks."

"Typical man. Doesn't appreciate the finer things in life," Jennifer said with a laugh.

"And you? What have you been up to?" This was Camilla, who selected a small Christmas cookie and nibbled at the edge.

Jennifer lowered her voice. "Derek and I ran into Joel the other day. He looked... really sad. I hated to see him like that."

"I think Renée leaving him kind of ran him through," Olivia said before she hurriedly added, "But he'll get through. I'm sure he's just surprised what it's like out there in the dating world."

"I feel like I got so lucky with Derek," Jennifer murmured just loud enough for them to hear. "But I can't help but feel guilty for it."

"Come on," Mila countered. "There's no feeling guilty. There's only being grateful. Haven't we been over this?"

A moment of silence passed over them. From the dining room came the sound of Isabelle in the midst of one of her college stories.

"And then he told me that he had to study? Again? I mean, I get that chemistry is maybe a little more intensive than other majors."

"That's just what he wants you to think," Stacy affirmed.

"Men are tricky. Who knows who was in the lab waiting for him," added Chelsea.

"I know! I had this nice, cozy high school relationship and had no idea what the wide world was all about," Isabelle grumbled.

"She has a whole lot to learn, doesn't she?" Mila breathed, just loud enough for the women in the kitchen to hear. "Unfortunately, I think I even have a lot more to learn, even at forty-one."

"Isn't that kind of a beautiful thing, though?" Jennifer asked. "We were once the girls in the next room, with our lives ahead of us. We still have lives ahead of us, God willing. But we also have all this life experience behind us. This rich texture."

Dinner was served at one: honeyed ham with mashed potatoes and gravy, roasted Brussels sprouts, buttermilk biscuits, salad, and pumpkin pie. The table wasn't quite big enough to accommodate all of them, which forced them to set up another table on the closed-in wrap-around porch, with its profound view of the Sound just beyond. The snow grew thicker, as though the house had been positioned inside a snow globe, so much so that as they dined, it became increasingly difficult to see the ocean.

"I do hope it's okay to drive home later," Ariane said to the table outside as she peered out.

"If not, everyone can sleep here," Jennifer countered. "There's enough blankets and pillows for everyone to collapse wherever they may. That's normally what happens after we eat too much, anyway."

Mila, Jennifer, Olivia, Camilla, Amelia, Hannah and Ariane sat around a different circular table and listened to the hubbub of conversation within. Jennifer was glad to have the natural light outside and the view of the curtain-thick sweep of the snow.

It felt like a different kind of Christmas, with Stacy's miscarriage and Mila's accident and Hannah's recent stint in the hospital. But it was true what Mila had said— gratitude was the key.

Midway through their meal, Hannah lifted her wine glass and cleared her throat. Slowly but surely, the girls' conversation dwindled out to make room for what this stranger wanted to say.

"I just have to tell you that this is a very different kind of Christmas for me." Hannah adjusted the green scarf around her neck distractedly. "I don't know why I'm still on this earth. I had a real hunch I wanted off of it. But somehow, through the kindness of some of the women at this table, I'm still here. The snow out across the Sound is some of the most miraculous snow I've seen in my life, and I feel very sure that I want to be around for a whole lot more snowfalls. I hope my friendship with all of you grows. And if it doesn't— if we go our separate ways— know that I am terribly grateful for the time we've spent together. It's meant the world to me and I just wanted you all to know that."

The other women at the table lifted their glasses to match Hannah's.

"You're so welcome here in our home," Ariane chimed in, giving Hannah her warmest smile.

"And in mine," Mila affirmed. "You've been a lifesaver for me, too." She then turned to meet each and every one of the other women's eyes. "And you. And you. And you." She said it all the way around the table until her eyes were heavy with tears. "I don't know how I would have lived through any of this without you."

It hit them all right then: only a few weeks before; they'd nearly lost their beloved Mila. Time had stood still as fate itself had hovered above the earth before making its ultimate decision.

They'd been allowed to keep Mila; they'd been allowed to hold onto the life they had together as a five-some.

But there was really no telling how much time on earth anyone had. That lesson seemed to come time and time again as the years passed.

After the meal, Jennifer piled the plates together and padded to the kitchen, where she scraped them clean and placed them gently in the dishwasher. In the living room, there came the sound of her son and Derek, each howling at a sports team on the television.

"Pull it together!"

"Come on!"

Jennifer grinned inwardly as she scrubbed her hands. They were the sounds of the vibrant souls she loved the most in the world. As she grew distracted with thought and the water rushed across her hands, strong arms wrapped around her stomach as a man placed his chin on her shoulder gently.

"Hey, beautiful," Derek breathed before he kissed her on the cheek.

Jennifer turned herself into him and lifted her chin. He shrieked playfully as she doused him with sink water. Neither cared, not really, as their lips found one another's and they hovered in the soft grey light of the kitchen as the radio played, "I'll Be Home for Christmas," a song that always seemed so sorrowful, yet seemed, in Jennifer's cherished life, always to be true.

Epilogue

One Month Later

"Ohh, Mila. I'm just not so sure about this." Hannah paced in the living room of Mila's house on Witchwood with her eyes focused on the ground. "I mean, I just haven't... I haven't even..."

"Gone on a date since before you married your husband?" Mila finished. "I figured as much."

"It's just that I don't really get the point," Hannah blurted as she yanked her head up. Her eyes were passionate and overly large, like those of a child. "I'm nearly sixty-five years old. Anyone in their sixties probably has buckets of money and all eyes on women half my age."

"This guy is seriously great," Jennifer affirmed from the opposite couch as she flipped through a magazine distractedly. "He's a friend of Derek's with plenty of money, yes, but he's not a particularly vain man and he likes a woman who can keep up with him intellectually."

"And he's a bit on the younger side..." Mila teased.

"Younger?" Hannah chirped. "I'm not a cougar!"

"Relax, Hannah. He's fifty-nine," Jennifer returned as she slapped her magazine off to the side. "He said he's free Friday for dinner before he heads back to the city on Saturday. Why don't you just try it? See what happens? If it's a no-go, then it's a no-go."

"You have nothing to lose," Mila told her as softly as she could, coaxing her. "Remember what we always say now. There's so much life to live."

"There's so much life to live," Hannah echoed.

"We're going to be late," Jennifer announced as she turned her wrist to catch the light of her wristwatch. Along with that turn, she flashed her engagement band— a new addition to the fourth finger as of only a few days before.

"I see you showing off over there," Mila said as she reached for her crutches and hauled herself upright.

"What do you mean?" Jennifer feigned innocence as she twirled her fingers through her red hair and flashed her left hand to and fro. "I just really don't know what I would have to show off?"

"Good grief," Hannah replied as she burst into laughter. "You have a good time at the rehabilitation clinic. As if you don't always."

Mila blushed as she hovered with her crutches for a moment before collapsing again in her wheelchair. Her strength had mounted day-by-day as she'd grown more accustomed to the crutches and her wobbly legs beneath her. Even still, Jack had said it would take time. "I guess I have nothing but time," Mila had told him in return.

Hannah slipped back into her car outside after a wave of her hand. Jennifer and Mila watched as she pulled out before they, too, piled into Mila's car.

"Do you miss her being around the house?" Jennifer asked.

"I do, actually," Mila replied. "But she likes her space with all her art and her photographs and her vinyl records. I have to respect that."

"She loves you so much, Mila," Jen offered then. "You're the daughter she always wanted."

Mila blushed as the feeling overtook her again. Sometimes, the love she felt for the beautiful people in her life felt overwhelming, like ocean waves crashing over her and disallowing her to breathe.

Up at the hospital, Jennifer wheeled Mila's wheelchair alongside Mila as Mila pushed herself forward on her crutches with an ease that surprised even Jennifer.

"You've gotten good at them," she said. "Do your legs feel stronger?"

"They do. But hasn't been that long..." Mila countered. "So I don't want to push it. Just maybe here to the door and then the chair."

But when they reached the door, it opened automatically to reveal none other than the handsome rehabilitation doctor, Jack Lawrence. Mila's heart shot into her throat at the sight of him.

"There she is. My top patient," he smiled as she entered.

As Mila hobbled through the door, she was reminded of long-ago mornings at Edgartown High School, when she'd entered in that cheerleading miniskirt and eight out of ten heads had turned with jealousy. That's how Jack made her feel.

She hadn't thought she'd ever feel that way again. It was miraculous.

"You want the chair?" Jennifer asked as she gestured toward Mila's now-forgotten wheelchair.

"Oh, what? Oh, no. I can make it."

Jennifer gave just the slightest of eye rolls as she witnessed Mila go full-on teenager. "Have fun," she said as Mila headed in after Doctor Jack.

After the traditional routine that Jack outlined for her every three days, Mila sat with her legs outstretched on the large patient chair so that Jack could assess her growing flexibility. For some reason, Mila thought this was a good time to tell him how flexible she'd been as a cheerleader.

"I was the most flexible of anyone else on the team," she explained brightly. "I could put both of my legs behind my head."

Jack laughed appreciatively. "I don't know if we can get you there by spring, but maybe by autumn?"

Mila blushed. "Will you still be my doctor in autumn?"

Jack's face fell into stoicism for the briefest of seconds before he said. "Well, I guess we'll see what kind of progress you make, won't we?"

What had Mila wanted him to say? Had she wanted him to propose a many-year-long journey toward wellness? Had she wanted him to propose marriage?

You have to walk before you can run, she told herself now as she assessed the strange scars across her naked legs.

Admittedly, they weren't as bad as she'd thought they

would be. They seemed to tell a story of survival, one she thought she rather liked. Who else could say they'd survived something like that? It had been a journey into the darkness of her soul and back again, like an epic written by Jules Verne.

When they were finished for the afternoon, Mila hovered on her crutches at the door, again like a teenager waiting for a boy to ask her to prom or something. Jack looked equally nervous. His blue eyes captivated her. They seemed as blue as the Nantucket Sound. He pressed open the door, which broke the spell only slightly, as Jennifer rushed up through the hallway with the wheelchair before her.

Mila wanted to tell her to stay back if only so she could have a few more beautiful moments of flirtation with Jack. Maybe it was all in her head. Maybe it wasn't. But did it really matter?

"Mila! We have to hurry!" Jennifer's voice rasped so much that Mila lost her balance on the crutches and catapulted herself into Jack Lawrence's arms.

"Woah!" Jack cried as he held onto her.

God, his arms were so comforting. Mila had forgotten what it felt like to be held like that. She'd forgotten what it felt to be safe in the warm arms of a man.

And Jack Lawrence was nothing if not a man.

"Mila! Amelia went into labor!" Jennifer cried as Jack eased Mila into the wheelchair again, a place she so desperately wanted to escape.

"Oh my gosh!" Mila draped her hand over her mouth. "Oh my gosh!"

Jack imitated them playfully. "Oh my gosh!" But his smile was infectious. "I guess you ladies had better go. She's one of your five-some, isn't she?"

"Indeed she is," Mila said. "You paid attention."

"It's part of my job to learn details about my patients," Jack told her sheepishly.

"Ah. I see."

Jennifer began to drag the wheelchair back as Jack hustled after her with the crutches in hand. Mila's eyes met with Jack's as laughter rolled over her. The moment seemed so outrageous and outside of time. She wanted to record all of it— every intimate and silly detail.

When they reached the hallway that led to Labor and Delivery, Jack pressed the crutches into Jennifer's arms and made eye contact with Mila all over again.

"By the way. About autumn," he stuttered.

"What about autumn?" Mila's lips twisted into a smile.

"I just think, you know. Maybe we won't have to meet in these sterile walls. But we could still work together. The football player and the cheerleader. Weren't we always supposed to work together? Although I guess we switched places. I'm more of the cheerleader as you head out there on the field."

"We could maybe work something out, Cheerleader," Mila returned softly as they shared a smile.

"Good."

"Good," she repeated back. She then swallowed the lump in her throat as she said, "But right now, me and my best friends have to welcome our new best friend into the world. It's kind of a big deal. So maybe... that date can wait?"

Jack's smile stretched across the entirety of his face. "Tell your new best friend welcome to the big, wide world. There's so much to see and so much to love, if only you give it a chance."

Jennifer wheeled Mila swiftly through the hallways after that as Mila cackled with delight.

"If only you give it a chance!" Jennifer repeated his words. "God, he loves you, Mila. But that's not new, is it?"

Mila shivered with joy. Despite the chill to the January air and the weight of the walking journey to come, there was a lightness to her, an assuredness that all would be all right as long as there was love between them. Very soon, Amelia would welcome a baby into the fold and finally, finally become a mother, after so much hope and so much heartache.

There was so much open to them— beauty and heartache and love and hope. They just had to be brave enough to experience all of it without holding themselves back. It was the Sisters of Edgartown's way.

Other Books by Katie

The Vineyard Sunset Series

Secrets of Mackinac Island Series

Sisters of Edgartown Series

A Katama Bay Series

A Mount Desert Island Series

Connect with Katie Winters

BookBub: www.bookbub.com/authors/katie-winters
Amazon: www.amazon.com/Katie-Winters/e/B08B1S7BBN
Facebook: www.facebook.com/authorkatiewinters/
Newsletter: www.subscribepage.com/kwsiguppage

To receive exclusive updates from Katie Winters please sign up to be on her Newsletter!

www.subscribepage.com/kwsiguppage

Made in the USA
Monee, IL
30 June 2022

98864218R00115